You can return this item to any library but please
note that not all libraries are open every day.
Items must be returned on or before the due date.
Failure to do so will result in overdue charges.
Items may be renewed unless requested by
another customer, in person or by telephone, on
two occasions only. Your membership card
number will be required.
Please look after this item – you may be charged
for any damage.

BOURNEMOUTH LIBRARIES
Headquarters: Leisure & Tourism Directorate
Town Hall, Bournemouth, BH2 6DY

He had to have one last look at his baby, Rosalie, he told himself, before this day came to an end.

When he gazed down into the cot his eyes widened. She was awake, smiling up at him as if she'd been waiting for him. Then she was pulling herself up by the cot sides and holding out her arms, and it was 'giving in' time. He couldn't hold out any longer. He lifted her out and cradled her to him, and as she cuddled close the barriers went down. He was the adoring father, holding the flesh of his flesh, and his heart sang with the joy of it.

Abigail Gordon loves to write about the fascinating combination of medicine and romance from her home in a Cheshire village. She is active in local affairs and is even called upon to write the script for the annual village pantomime! Her eldest son is a hospital manager and helps with all her medical research. As part of a close-knit family, she treasures having two of her sons living close by and the third one not too far away. This also gives her the added pleasure of being able to watch her delightful grandchildren growing up.

Recent titles by the same author:

HER SURGEON BOSS
THE DOCTOR'S BABY BOND
THE SURGEON'S FAMILY WISH
THE POLICE SURGEON'S RESCUE
THE GP'S SECRET

A SURGEON'S MARRIAGE WISH

BY
ABIGAIL GORDON

MILLS & BOON®

First published in Great Britain 2005
Harlequin Mills & Boon Limited,
Eton House, 18-24 Paradise Road, Richmond, Surrey TW9 1SR

© Abigail Gordon 2005

ISBN 0 263 18738 1

Set in Times Roman 10½ on 12¼ pt.
07-0805-47591

Printed and bound in Great Britain
by Antony Rowe Ltd, Chippenham, Wiltshire

CHAPTER ONE

IT HAD had been one of the blackest days of her life, Kerry thought as she drove home in the warm summer night. On the trauma unit on the top floor of a big London hospital it was nothing new for the team up there to be fighting to save the lives of the seriously injured brought to them off the streets of the city below. But never before had they had to battle to save one of their own.

They had been calming down and clearing up after hours of surgery on a badly injured workman from a building site, and after transferring him into Intensive Care with a reasonable chance of recovery, had been wondering who or what would be next.

The familiar whirring of helicopter rotors hadn't been long in coming and as the helicopter had landed on the helipad outside, the expression on the face of the doctor on board had been grim, to say the least.

'It's the chief,' he cried as he flung open the doors. 'We need to get him on to the table fast. His heart has stopped twice on the way here.'

'You don't mean Daniel!' Kerry cried in horror as they all rushed towards the stretcher that was being carefully unloaded.

'Yes. It's Mr Jefferson,' she was told tersely. 'He was jostled by a gang of louts in the city centre and knocked over. He cracked his head on the pavement.'

They were good, the team who fought for the lives

of the injured amongst the rooftops, and in the hours that followed they'd never been better, but there'd been a massive brain haemorrhage and the pleasant, elderly genius who had welded together the team of surgeons, anaesthetists, radiologists, theatre nurses and others to make one of the best trauma units in the land slipped away from them.

There wasn't a dry eye in the place, but Kerry's grief was the greatest as Daniel Jefferson hadn't just been her boss. He'd been her much-loved father-in-law who had stood by her when her marriage to his son had broken up.

And now he was gone. The man who had taken her into his home and helped her in every way he'd been able to without making judgements or taking sides. He'd been there for her when the baby had been born, and because she'd begged him not to tell Piers he had a daughter he'd reluctantly agreed, making no comment when she'd said tightly that if he did know her husband would probably think the child was someone else's.

Looking down at Rosalie, Daniel must have thought that was very unlikely as the little one had the same dark eyes and hair as her father, the firm mouth and the long tapering fingers that were a boon to a good surgeon.

But he'd known the depth of his daughter-in-law's hurt and had gone along with her wishes, hoping that one day the mess his son and Kerry had got themselves into would sort itself out. There'd been faults on both sides and they should accept it.

As the house that had been her home for almost two years came into view, Kerry's thoughts were on

Rosalie, sleeping the sleep of the innocent in her pretty nursery and quite unaware that they might soon have to be on the move once more.

With his father gone, the house would belong to Piers, and if she found him as unflinching now as he'd been before, a very awkward situation was going to arise when he found her living there.

But none of that mattered at the moment. His father was dead. She had to let Piers know and had no idea where he might be.

Kerry worked three days each week on the trauma unit, and during that time her friend Lizzie looked after Rosalie for her. She was a freelance artist and the money she earned from the child care helped to keep her solvent.

She was curled up on the couch, waiting to go home, when Kerry appeared and shot bolt upright the moment she saw her friend's expression.

'You look awful!' she exclaimed. 'Whatever is wrong?'

'Daniel is dead.' Kerry explained in a voice thickening with tears. As she described what had happened Lizzie's face went pale with horror.

'Does Piers know?'

Kerry shook her head.

'How can he? No one knows where he is.'

'Surely his father would have known.'

'Possibly, but he never said anything. I'll have to go through his papers and see if I can find an address as there is a funeral to arrange and that is Piers's responsibility. He won't want me interfering in their affairs.'

'Do you think he knows that you have been living in his father's house?'

'I have no idea.'

'So he's still not been in touch.'

'No. His pride and arrogance would prevent him. I haven't had a word from him since he left me.'

'It's such a shame.' Lizzie said gently. 'You two were fantastic together. I would have said your marriage was rock solid. You both knew what you wanted out of life and it always seemed as if it was each other above all else.'

'Yes, maybe so,' Kerry agreed bleakly, 'but we are both stubborn and stupid with it, and look where it's got us. There is never a day goes by that I don't think about him, wonder where he is, what he's doing. But he didn't trust me, Lizzie. He thought that because I was defending Danny Cosgrove I was having an affair with him, when it was all just a matter of principle that I was getting steamed up about. And the awful thing is that Piers wasn't wrong about one thing. Danny wasn't up to the standards of a busy A and E department. I realised that when it was too late.'

'And have you told Piers that?'

'No. How could I when I don't know where he is? And in any case, he's the one who walked out. Not me.'

Obviously feeling that a change of subject was called for, Lizzie's next comment was about the present.

'Do you want me to stay with you tonight?' she offered. 'I've nothing planned.'

Kerry shook her head.

'No. I'll be all right. You've been here long

enough. I'll go and peep at my daughter in a moment. Has she been all right?'

'Of course. Little Miss Beautiful and I played with her toys this morning, then she had her lunch and after that a nap. We went to the park in the afternoon, followed by tea, bathtime and bed. You really are denying that man of yours a lot of joy in keeping his daughter a secret.'

'I know. Don't think I don't have my guilty moments. I do. Lots of them. And if he'd ever taken the trouble to get in touch I would have told him that we have a child. But all of that is going to be in the past now. Once I've managed to contact him he's bound to find out about her, and what will happen then I daren't think about.'

When Lizzie had gone Kerry searched through the papers in her father-in-law's desk but found no address for Piers. The rest of the house yielded no contact information either, and perching herself on the bottom step of the stairs she pondered on what to do next.

Daniel's solicitor might know where Piers was, she thought suddenly. If his father *had* known where he was, surely he would have given Ian that sort of information in the event of something like today's tragic events occurring.

The two men had been friends for years, and in any case he needed to know that Daniel was dead. He would be in charge of his affairs and someone she could turn to until Piers showed up. Then she would bow out gracefully, leaving him to arrange the funeral of the man who had been there for her when his son hadn't.

Ian Sangster wasn't in, but his wife was, and when Kerry asked if they had an address for Piers there was an awkward silence at the other end of the line.

I have an urgent reason for asking, Mrs Sangster,' she told her. 'Otherwise I wouldn't be troubling you.'

'Piers is here,' she said at last. 'He flew in from New Zealand this morning and is due to meet up with his father tonight.'

Kerry felt that if she hadn't still been sitting at the bottom of the stairs her legs would have given way as she tried to absorb what the other woman was saying.

'Piers is with you?' she croaked. 'Thank goodness! I'm desperate to speak to him. Could you get him to come to the phone, please?'

'I will ask him, my dear,' she said doubtfully. 'Will you hold on for a moment?'

When the voice that she hadn't heard for almost two years spoke in her ear, Kerry flinched.

'Yes? What's the problem?' Piers asked in a tone that was neither cold nor warm, just flat. She was tempted to tell him the awful tidings there and then instead of to his face, as he deserved to be told, but she couldn't be so cruel.

'I need to speak to you about something very urgent regarding your father. I'm at his house. Could you come round here, please?'

'We spoke on the phone only yesterday,' he said in the same flat tone. 'I can't imagine that much has changed since then.'

'It has, I can assure you,' Kerry told him through dry lips.

'All right. I'll be round shortly,' he said in a more

responsive tone, and without giving her time to reply he went off the line.

One's whole world could change in a matter of seconds, Kerry thought grimly, let alone days. There is grief in store for you, Piers, and how I wish there wasn't.

She'd loved Daniel, but Piers loved him more. The man she'd married was a man of passion who kept the faith and had little patience with those who didn't, which he'd decided included herself. And now they had been brought back into each other's company through one of the saddest of life's occurrences and her skin was clammy with dread at the thought of what was to come.

Yet there was anticipation in her, too. She was actually going to see Piers in the flesh for the first time in many lonely months, and whatever the outcome of their meeting she wouldn't want to have missed that.

Kerry had met him when they'd both been working in a hospital up north. She'd been a theatre nurse, as she still was, and, having followed in his father's footsteps, Piers had been in charge of the hospital's accident and emergency department.

The attraction between the totally dedicated, dark-haired doctor and the serene blonde nurse had been overpowering, and wedding bells hadn't been far behind.

It had been bliss until Piers's devotion to the job and intolerance of anyone he'd felt hadn't been up to standard had caused Kerry to befriend a hapless young registrar who hadn't been able to do anything right for Piers, and a small crack had appeared in her relationship with her husband.

She'd known that Piers had once lost a patient through crass negligence on the part of one of his staff and had never forgotten it, but she had still thought that his treatment of the young registrar had been over the top.

She'd often thought since that their marriage might still have survived if Piers had been less arrogant and demanding, but the more he'd ranted about her friendship with Danny Cosgrove, the more she'd stood by him, and soon they had disagreed on almost everything. Small irritations that once they would have laughed at became disputes that neither would give in on.

Kerry had been dismayed at the way their first real misunderstanding had turned into a major conflict. She would never have believed she could be so stubborn and that Piers could be so unflinching over something that should not have intruded into their private lives. But it had, and as the days had gone by with a mixture of cold silences and heated confrontations she had felt that he had wanted to control her, that he had been possessive and jealous when he had had no cause to be and in the process her independence had been threatened.

She was of a milder, less forceful nature than Piers, but that didn't mean she was going to be walked all over, she had told herself, even though she had adored him.

As the weeks had passed, she had seen how their marriage was crumbling and knew that they were finding out aspects of each other's characters that they hadn't been aware of during the first heady bliss of matrimony. She had also realised that her determination to defend Danny wasn't the cause of their disagreements. Rather it had been the trigger to something that would have happened sooner or later.

It had all come to a head on the day that Piers found her accepting a comforting hug from the young registrar, and his anger and pride had turned the crack into a great divide when he had accused her of all sorts of hurtful things that weren't true.

Before she had had time to come to terms with that last awful quarrel, always quick to act, he had resigned from the hospital, packed his bags and left, and she hadn't seen him since.

When his father had discovered that she was carrying his son's child the kindly widower had persuaded her to move to London to live with him. He had found her the job on the trauma unit where he was the head, and that was how it had been until today.

The doorbell rang and she started to shake. In all the times she'd imagined coming face to face with Piers again it had never been like this, with the burden of such sad news sitting heavily upon her shoulders. But it had to be faced, she told herself, and the sooner it was said the sooner she might know where she stood with him…if anywhere.

He'd never expected it to be like this when he saw Kerry again, Piers was thinking as he waited for her to open the door. His idea had been to get settled into the new job and *then* see how the land lay.

He'd flown over a couple of months ago in answer to his father's letter telling him that he was intending to take early retirement and would feel more content if his son was back practicing medicine in England during his remaining years.

'One of our surgeons on the trauma team is moving out of the area shortly,' he'd written, 'so that will be the first vacancy, and mine, which isn't yet official, will be the second. Why don't you apply for his job?'

There had been an appeal in the letter that he hadn't been able to ignore, and there had also been the thought that going back to the country of his birth would take him a lot nearer to his estranged wife than he'd been in many long months. So he'd been over, been interviewed, and a week ago had been told that the appointment was his if he wanted it.

Did he want it? he'd asked himself. Of course he did. He'd been doing a similar thing in New Zealand, but it had been just a matter of living for the job, as there'd been nothing else to live for with Kerry out of his life. And now he'd got the chance to come back to his roots and find out what was happening in his wife's life.

His father had said that his coming retirement was a closely guarded secret. That not even Kerry, who was staying with him, knew about it. But there were other closely guarded secrets that Daniel had kept quiet about, and one of them was that she was also a member of the trauma team and would be working with Piers when he came. That was something he had yet to find out.

It hadn't occurred to Piers that his father might have some little scheme of his own in mind. He'd thought that it was a case of Daniel looking after his son's career and wanting him back in England. He didn't know that Daniel had decided it was time that

Piers got to know his daughter and if her stubborn parents weren't ready to sort out their lives, he was. Daniel had never dreamt that his plotting might turn out to be part of his legacy to them both.

The summer night was drawing in and in the fading light his face looked hawk-like and haggard, but when Piers stepped into the lighted hallway Kerry saw that the eyes were the same, dark and challenging, and she sensed that beneath the surface the vitality that had drawn her to him like a magnet in those early days was still there.

'Hello, Piers,' she said, trying to keep her voice steady. 'I'm sorry I had to drag you away from the Sangsters, but I had no choice. If you'll come through to the sitting room, I'll explain why.'

He shrugged and as she turned to lead the way he followed without speaking until they were in the other room and then, making no effort to sit down, he asked abruptly, 'So what's this about Dad? Where is he? What's the panic for?'

'He died this afternoon, Piers,' she said gently, and watched the blood drain from his face to leave him looking even more drawn.

'No!' he cried. 'It can't be true! Not my dad. He was invincible!'

'Not against a gang of hooligans in the city centre. They pushed him down and he cracked his head on the pavement. The helicopter brought him to his own trauma unit but it was too late to save him. The head injuries were too severe.'

Tears were streaming down his hollow cheeks and she ached to hold him close and comfort him, but she was afraid that he might repulse her and she couldn't cope with that, not tonight of all nights. So she tried to change the subject.

'How do you come to be in London? I was amazed when Mrs Sangster said you were at their place. I was anticipating having difficulty finding you and you were just a couple of miles away.'

He cleared his throat and told her tonelessly, 'I've been working abroad but, having been offered a plum job in London, I've come back.'

The implications of the calm announcement turned her legs to jelly, 'Why are you staying with the Sangsters?' she croaked. 'Surely your father would have expected you to stay with him.'

The old sardonic gleam was in his eyes as he explained, '*You* are living here. Does that answer the question?'

She looked down at the carpet so he wouldn't see the hurt that his words had caused and told him, 'Maybe I am, but you have more right to be here than I have.'

He didn't dispute that, just commented, 'It seemed like the sensible thing to do. I've known the Sangsters for years. But surely there are more important things to discuss than where I'm staying. Where is Dad now?'

'In the hospital mortuary.'

'So that needs to be rectified immediately and funeral arrangements got under way. Have you done anything towards that?'

Kerry swallowed hard. She knew him so well. He was in control now. Had a grip on his grief. There would be no more signs of weakness, not in front of her anyway.

'No.' she told him. 'I didn't think it was my place. But I will do anything I can to help. I loved your father. He was good to me when I needed a friend. I won't ever forget his kindness.'

She watched the harsh lines of his face soften.

'Hmm. That was like Dad. Though I wouldn't have thought he needed to take *you* under his wing. From what I remember, you were protective of your independence to an absurd degree.'

That was before I discovered I was carrying your child, she thought. The child you know nothing about, who is sleeping upstairs. Yet even as the words formed themselves in her mind she knew them to be wrong in part. Rosalie was not asleep. She was crying loudly in the room above them.

She watched his glance move upwards and waited.

'That noise,' he said. 'It sounds like a child crying.'

'It is,' she told him quietly, and saw her dream fade of one day, as a picture of composed motherhood, presenting their beautiful daughter to her father. Rosalie was a contented, bright-eyed toddler who hardly ever cried, but not tonight. Something had obviously brought her out of her sleep.

'So?' he questioned guardedly.

'So, you are about to be introduced to your daughter, Piers.'

The little one's sobs were increasing in volume and she was desperate to get to her to find out what was wrong, but the look on his face was keeping her rooted to the spot.

'You are telling me that we have a child,' he said

slowly. Kerry nodded mutely. 'And that neither you nor my father thought fit to inform me of that.'

'I made him promise not to tell you. I didn't want you coming back to me because you felt duty bound, and he didn't know where you were in any case.'

She was edging towards the stairs and to do that she had to pass him. When she drew level his arm sprang out and he pulled her towards him until they were touching, and with her breasts up against his chest he said harshly, 'That's a lame excuse! But as the moment is upon us, perhaps you'll introduce us.'

She nodded again and with heart thumping led the way upstairs, with Piers following her like someone in a trance.

The night was humid. Rosalie was too warm. Her hair lay damply upon her brow and red-faced and snuffly she was at her least appealing as she protested at the discomfort that had brought her out of a sound sleep. As Kerry lifted her out of the cot she said, 'This is Rosalie, Piers, your daughter, normally a happy little soul, but not tonight, it would seem. Do you want to hold her while I straighten the covers?' she asked awkwardly.

He shook his head.

'No,' he said, unable to keep the bitterness out of his voice. 'A fretful child doesn't take kindly to being handled by a *stranger*.'

Kerry felt her sick anxiety increase.

Once in her mother's arms Rosalie's sobs subsided and the dark eyes so like his were observing her father. She smiled and held out the small teddy bear that she always slept with. His face twisted.

'How could you?' he choked. 'How could you not tell me I had a daughter?'

'How could *you* leave me without caring enough to find out!' she flashed back angrily. 'And before you start questioning if she's yours, take a good look at her and you'll have your answer.'

She was talking to his departing back. Piers was going down the stairs two at a time and seconds later she heard the front door slam behind him.

A gentle dabbing with cool water of her hot little face and a change into fresh pyjamas and within minutes Rosalie was asleep again, cherubic and peaceful once more.

But there was no relief to be had from Kerry's distress. In the course of a day she'd lost her much-loved father-in-law, met up with Piers again and seen it as maybe the only good thing to have come out of the tragedy, only to have his introduction to his daughter thrust upon her, when she'd so much wanted it to be at a different time and place.

What now? she kept asking herself as the night hours crept slowly by.

What now indeed?

Piers was in a state of aching disbelief as he drove to the hospital to see his father, for what would be one of the last times, and to arrange for him to be removed to more suitable surroundings until the funeral could take place.

Tonight he had discovered in the most painful way that one life had been taken away and another, that he'd known nothing of, had come into existence during his lonely separation, and no one had thought fit to tell him. Neither his wife nor his father.

But on the heels of that thought came the memory of what Kerry had said. They hadn't known where he was. It had only been during the last two months that he had surfaced from his self-imposed exile in New Zealand, and even if she *had* known where he was, would Kerry have wanted to get in touch after the way he'd treated her?

That he'd left her pregnant was the last thing he had expected. During those last miserable weeks they'd only slept together once. A brief passionate reconciliation that had fizzled out again, neither of them wanting to give way on what they had seen as their principles.

He was a fool, he told himself. A proud and arrogant fool. And where had it got him? He'd missed out on the birth of that beautiful child who had smiled at him through her tears and offered him her little teddy bear, almost as if she had sensed that a peace offering had been called for.

He'd wept for his father in front of Kerry. He hadn't wanted her to see him weep for his daughter, too, and he'd rushed out of the house before he had.

Now he wanted to go back and pick up that sweet, dark-eyed cherub and never let her go, but his duty to his father came first and tomorrow was another day. A day that he was going to be facing with a great many conflicting emotions.

Kerry had looked older. She'd been a serene twenty-seven-year-old when they'd first met. She had smiled a lot and had been capable of a great tenderness that had all been for him, until she'd got the ridiculous fixation about protecting Danny Cosgrove and he, Piers, had become the bad guy.

He'd seen back there at the house that she was nervous and strained, that the serenity had gone, just the same as he'd lost the vibrance that had attracted *her* to *him*. For the last couple of years he'd done the job that he loved with a mechanical sort of perfection, always ready to do extra duties because there had been nothing else in his life, and unknown to him she'd been coping with the responsibility of bringing up their child while he had been sulking far away, wrapped up in his own hurts.

Thankfully Kerry hadn't been alone. His father had been there on the sidelines like the rock that he had been, and how he wished he could thank him for it face to face, instead of only being able to think it.

Two months ago, unable to bear the separation any longer, he'd phoned his father. Daniel had been overjoyed to hear his voice, but when he'd asked about Kerry, desperate for news of her, all he'd been told was that she was fine and staying with Daniel at the London house.

Hot on the heels of the phone call had come his father's letter with news of the coming vacancy in the trauma unit where he was senior surgeon and explaining that he was planning early retirement and would dearly like to have his son back home.

That Daniel might be involved in some subtle planning of his own hadn't occurred to him until today. But now it seemed as if his father's intention might have been to encourage him to go after the job that would bring him back into their lives and at the same time present the opportunity for him to meet his daughter.

It had been obvious that Kerry had known nothing about what was going on in the background. She'd been dumbstruck to find him at the Sangsters' place and must have been dreading having to break the news of his father's death to him. But even something as terrible as that had come second to what had happened in the nursery upstairs.

'Do you want to hold her?' she'd asked.

Had he wanted to hold his daughter? he thought bitterly. Of course he had. But he'd said no. Been his usual ungracious self because his arms had felt like leaden weights and he hadn't been able to bear Kerry to see the state he'd been in.

His father's face was composed in death. As Piers looked down at him he imagined that he saw complacency there, as if he'd accomplished what he'd set out to do on earth before moving on to higher things.

They'd lost his mother with heart failure when he himself had been in his early teens, and Daniel had made sure he had been there for him every step of the way. Even when he'd been bent on destroying his marriage he'd stood by him, but because he'd loved his daughter-in-law, too, his father had never taken sides and Piers knew just how hard that must have been.

I'm back, Dad,' he told him gravely, 'and I've just met my daughter. Is that what it was all about, me being given the opportunity to find out that I'm a father? You knew, didn't you, that no matter how I feel towards Kerry, now that I've seen my child I'm not going to disappear again? I'm going to take my rightful place in their lives, and if my wife isn't happy about that she and I are going to have to live with it.'

He bent and placed his lips against his father's cold brow. 'Goodbye, Dad. Thanks for all you've done for them…and for me. I wish I could have said all of this to you when you were alive, but I denied myself the opportunity.'

At eight o'clock the next morning the doorbell rang again and Kerry knew that it was Piers. She wouldn't have been surprised if he'd come back in the middle of the night after leaving in such a state, but it seemed that he had restrained himself until then.

'I'm back,' he said flatly when she opened the door to him.

'Yes, so I see,' she said quietly, aware of Rosalie banging a plastic spoon on the tray of her high chair in the kitchen. Here comes the next hurdle, she thought.

'Rosalie is having her breakfast,' she said, trying to sound calm.

'Fine,' he replied. 'Am I allowed to watch?'

Ignoring the sarcasm, she said, 'Yes, of course you are. Whatever your feelings are towards me, I am extremely relieved that you've discovered that you have a daughter.'

He was striding into the kitchen and said dryly with a backward glance, 'It certainly qualifies as one of the world's best-kept secrets.'

'As were your whereabouts,' she parried defensively, and then wished she hadn't.

Their differences had to be put to one side, she told

herself. At least until the funeral was over, and with that in mind she asked, 'Did you go to see your father last night?'

'Yes,' he said curtly. 'He will be in the undertaker's care by now. Dad looked very peaceful. It was hard to tell that he'd suffered such serious injuries.'

'Yes, we did our best to cover them up,' she said sadly.

His gaze had been on Rosalie, happily spooning up her cereal in a hit-and-miss sort of fashion, but he whirled round to face her when he heard that.

'We? What had *you* to do with his treatment?'

So his father hadn't told him, she thought dismally. Piers didn't know that she was employed on the same trauma unit as Daniel had been. Something else to cringe over in the telling.

'I was there doing my job. I'm a part-time theatre nurse on the same unit, and was on duty when they brought him in. It would seem that is something else that you weren't aware of. Your father didn't just house me. He found me employment, too.'

'I don't believe it!' he cried in amazement. 'What next? Dad really was playing it close to his chest. He wrote and told me there was a vacancy coming up for a surgeon on his trauma team and persuaded me to apply for it, but he didn't tell me that you would be part of it. I'm due to start next week, so we're going to be working together again.'

There was no pleasure in his tone and, just as surprised as he, she protested, 'I knew nothing about any of this. I didn't know you'd been in touch. I was amazed to find you at the Sangsters', and like yourself had no idea that Daniel was arranging it so that we would be working together. I do hope you believe me.'

He shrugged and turned back to observe Rosalie again. There was hunger in his eyes as he looked at his daughter. A twist to the mouth that had once mesmerised her with its kisses and misery washed over her. Piers was back in her life but so far there was little joy in it. Was he feeling that he'd been brought back under false pretences?

If the expression on his face was anything to go by, it wasn't going to matter if he did. He'd seen his daughter and, knowing the measure of the man, he wasn't going to budge from her side now that he had, no matter what he had to put up with from her.

'I only work three days each week,' she said into the silence that had fallen.

'And who looks after our child during that time?' he asked immediately.

She almost smiled. He was still the same bossy boots. Into basics with no messing.

'You remember my friend Lizzie? She was a theatre nurse like me when we worked up north. Well, she gave up nursing to become an artist and she arrives at half past seven in the morning to see to Rosie and leaves when I get home at night. Does that satisfy you?'

'I'll let you know when I've seen her in action,' he said as he gently lifted one of Rosalie's dark curls. 'And what about today? Do you have to report for duty?'

'No, and I've taken leave for the rest of the week anyway, after having to watch my father-in-law die and not knowing if I would be able to find his son.'

'Yes, I'm sure that would be enough to demoralise anyone,' he said stiffly.

She wished he'd spare her the polite commiserations. She knew he didn't care a damn about her feelings.

We need to talk,' she told him in a tone to match his. 'Do you want me to move out of here after the funeral? I need to know soon if you do, so that I can find somewhere suitable for Rosalie and myself.'

If he'd been the composed one before, he wasn't now. She watched his jaw go slack and knew he hadn't been expecting her to take that sort of initiative.

'What, and take our daughter to live in some poky flat?'

'But the house belongs to you now.'

'So does she. If you think I'm going to let her out of my sight now, you are very much mistaken.'

'I would let you know where to find us.'

'I want you *both* here. Obviously Rosalie needs *you.*'

She was angry now. Since he'd arrived she'd been so careful not to cause friction, but that last comment to the effect that *she* would be there on sufferance because of their daughter had hit hard. He was still the same, she thought. Arrogant and demanding. Nothing had changed.

'You've got that right!' she cried. 'Rosalie *does* need *me*. She goes nowhere without me. So just bear that in mind if you feel inclined to start throwing your weight about!'

CHAPTER TWO

HE WAS getting it all wrong again, Piers thought as he took her anger on board. Better stay away from personal matters and concentrate on the practicalities of the situation regarding his father's death. There would be time to talk about themselves when he had been laid to rest.

'I'll fetch my stuff round this afternoon,' he said, letting Kerry's remarks pass without comment.

'You're moving in here, then?'

'Yes. I'll be able to keep a better grip on Dad's affairs if I do.'

He didn't tell her that now he'd discovered he had a daughter he couldn't bear to be away from her for a second longer than he needed to be.

'Shall I change the sheets in your father's room, then?' she asked without meeting his gaze.

Piers shook his head.

'No. Let's leave Dad's things as they are for the moment. I'll move into the spare room. The bed was always made up in there in case of emergency. Is it still?'

'Yes,' she told him, thinking bleakly that they were behaving like polite acquaintances instead of the people they'd once been. The nurse and the doctor who had been so in love they'd expected to be together for ever. But they hadn't reckoned with the havoc that two stubborn personalities could bring, and now they were paying the price.

Kerry was aware that Piers hadn't yet touched Rosalie, except for gently wrapping a strand of her hair around his finger. It wasn't in keeping with the way she'd expected him to act. She'd thought he would have swept their child up into his arms and smothered her with kisses, but on second thoughts, would he?

Would he want to give *her* the satisfaction of watching him turn into an adoring father within the space of twenty-four hours when he'd been denied the little one's presence for almost two years?

He was a passionate man. No one knew that better than she, but he was also proud, and the hurt, she'd done him by not letting him know of Rosalie's birth must be like salt on an open wound.

But she'd been hurt, too. Accused of unfaithfulness without being given the chance to defend herself, and then having to come to terms with the fact that her friendship with Danny Cosgrove *had* been a mistake. But by then it had been too late to admit it. Piers had gone and neither his father nor herself had known where he was…

'I'm going to spend the morning in the study,' he was saying, 'so don't let me interfere with your routine.' And with a long level look he left them to their own devices.

If they were going to be keeping up this sort of stilted politeness for any length of time she would go crazy, Kerry thought as she cleared away the breakfast things.

She *would* have to put the washer on, go food shopping, but only because she had no choice if they were to have clean clothes and food on the table. But if Piers thought she was going to be tuned into those sort of things with all that was in her mind, he was mistaken. The happenings of the previous day had left her in a state of high tension and there was more to come. Soon they would be working together on the unit if he didn't decide to give it a miss.

She was on the point of taking Rosalie to the shops when Lizzie rang, concerned to know what was happening.

'Piers is here,' Kerry told her in a low voice.

'I don't believe it!' her friend said in amazement. 'Where was he?'

'Staying with his father's solicitor. Piers has been working in New Zealand but is now back home and—wait for it—about to fill a vacancy on the trauma team…if he can stand working with me.'

'So nothing has changed?'

'No. Nothing has changed. We're like strangers.'

'Where would Dad keep his papers regarding his employment with the hospital trust?' Piers asked suddenly from behind her, and Kerry almost dropped the phone. He would have heard her discussing him, she thought miserably, and *that* wasn't going to help matters.

'In the wall safe in his bedroom, I would think,' she told him. To Lizzie, she said, 'I'll ring you this evening, when it's quieter.'

'You had your life all nicely organised here, didn't you?' he said dryly as she put the phone down. 'With Dad and Rosalie, and a good friend on the sidelines to take over when she was needed. My coming back is going to mess it all up, isn't it?'

'Only time will tell,' she said, not meeting his gaze.

She was apprehensive, anxious, in a state of shock, and yet beneath it all she was becoming alive again. Just the sight of him had been enough to make her blood surge and her heart beat faster.

Yet the ache for all that was gone wasn't going to go away—their love for each other, the joys of family life that they'd missed out on because of Piers's absence. As Rosalie began to fidget in her pram, Kerry managed a wintry smile.

'Maybe I wanted my life messed up. Has that occurred to you?' And off she went into the summer morning, relieved to be away from the sorrow that filled the house and the man who had been forced back into her life whether he wanted it or not.

It had been a strange, unreal sort of day, Kerry thought as she prepared to bath Rosalie that evening. Piers had spent most of the time on the phone accepting condolences from his father's many friends and associates and finalising the funeral arrangements, while she had gone through the motions of the routine that he'd mentioned with little enthusiasm.

The police had been round to say that they were still looking for the culprits, who had disappeared with all speed once they'd seen the results of their behaviour. It would seem that the incident had lasted only a matter of seconds but in that time a respected surgeon had received injuries from which he hadn't recovered.

As the hours had gone by, Piers's expression had

become more strained and bleached-looking. She'd longed to offer comfort. Hold him close and tell him that he wasn't alone. That she would support him in whatever way he wanted.

Losing Daniel in such tragic circumstances put their own self-inflicted problems into perspective. But would he accept her support if she offered it? They were together again in a strange family sort of setting, but it was of a frail substance, like gossamer over barbed wire.

She'd cooked a meal of sorts and they'd sat down together with Rosalie at her most enchanting in her high chair beside them. How could he resist the thought of the little one's smooth, softness up against him? Kerry thought as she watched him from beneath lowered lids. Yet he still hadn't touched her. Don't take your pique out on our baby, Piers, she prayed silently.

When they'd eaten he'd gone back into the study. The phone calls were still coming through but not to such a degree, and Kerry wondered how they were going to get through the evening. Was he going to stay in there for ever?

As she lowered Rosalie gently into the bath water, his shadow fell across them and she looked up and asked, 'Do you want to take over?'

He shook his head. 'Too much to do.'

Yet he stayed there when she started gently soaping and rinsing, and when she lifted Rosalie out into a big white towel he was still watching.

Piers just didn't want to be involved, did he? she thought soberly, and *she* was to blame for that. She should have searched until she'd found him when

Rosalie had been born, not kept their daughter to her-self out of a pique of her own.

He was still closeted in the study when she was ready to go to bed, and before going upstairs she tapped on the door and went in.

'Yes?' he said flatly, without looking up.

'Stop it!' she cried as grief and tiredness took over. 'Stop treating me like this. I'm not to blame for you having to come back into this situation and neither is Rosalie. Once the funeral is over, we're going, whether you like it or not!'

'Have you finished?' he asked grimly when she paused for breath.

'Yes. I have.' And turning, she left him to his thoughts, whatever they were.

Piers knew that he had her confused. That Kerry didn't understand why he was holding back from Rosalie. He thought his daughter was the most beau-tiful thing he'd ever seen. Every time he saw her he went weak with love. There was no way they were going to walk out of his life as Kerry had just threat-ened they would. But he was holding back.

His heart was already in the keeping of the tiny hands that had held out the teddy bear to him in those unbelievable first moments of meeting. But if he let himself become enslaved, where would it leave him if it didn't work out a second time? The agony of another break-up would be a thousand times worse than the first, now that he knew he had a daughter.

It was later, much later, when *he* decided to call it a day. There were no sounds coming from Kerry's room when he reached the upstairs landing, and after hesitating for a moment Piers moved noiselessly towards the nursery.

He *had* to have one last look at Rosalie, he told himself, before this ghastly day came to an end. When he gazed down into the cot his eyes widened. She was awake, smiling up at him as if she'd been waiting for him. Then she was pulling herself up by the cot sides and holding out her arms, and it was 'giving in' time. He couldn't hold out any longer.

He lifted her out and cradled her to him and as she cuddled close the barriers went down. He was the adoring father, holding the flesh of his flesh, and his heart sang with the joy of it.

Kerry had fallen into an exhausted doze the moment she'd laid her head on the pillow, as if her mind could take no more, but it was not to last. She was brought out of it by the sound of childish laughter and the deeper tones of Piers's voice.

Unbelieving, she eased herself carefully out of bed and tiptoed towards the nursery. As she hesitated in the doorway she saw that her prayers had been answered. Father and daughter were getting to know each other.

Piers looked up and saw her standing there, slender, golden haired...and anxious in a sensible cotton nightdress. Raising dark brows, he asked, 'So what can we do for *you*?'

'Nothing,' she said quietly. 'Just carry on as you are doing, but make sure that Rosalie has gone back to sleep before *you* settle down for the night.'

'Of course,' he replied, and leaving him to his special moment she went back to bed and slept, knowing that at least one of the things that had been breaking her heart had righted itself.

The funeral was over and the uncertain future lay ahead. Neither of them had referred again to the matters that plagued the other. Kerry hadn't mentioned moving out again and Piers was giving no inkling as to whether he was still joining the trauma team the following Monday.

'I've ordered just one funeral car for the three of us,' he'd told her the morning after the midnight miracle. 'The other mourners will be using their own transport.'

'Are you sure that you want me with you?' she'd asked uncomfortably.

'It's what Dad would want,' he'd told her. 'His family showing a united front. What *we* want comes second.'

'Fine,' she'd agreed, accepting the cold comfort of his reasoning and thinking that the day when *she* was loved like her daughter was going to be a long time coming...if ever.

But at least Piers was starting to be a father to their daughter. She offered up thanks for that every time she saw him with Rosalie. He would stand on his head and sing the national anthem in Spanish for her if the child knew the words to ask him to, she thought gratefully. And in the meantime she herself was putting her own affairs to one side until such time as he was ready to talk.

Because talk they must...and soon.

The opportunity came on the evening of the funeral. The mourners, who had all been invited back to the house for refreshments, had gone. The caterers had cleared up after them, and the feeling of anticlimax that often followed such events was strong.

When Rosalie had been settled for the night Piers said, 'We need to get out of here for a while. It's beginning to feel claustrophobic. Does your friend Lizzie live near enough to come round at short notice?'

'Yes, she's only a couple of miles away,' Kerry told him, surprised at the suggestion. 'Do you want me to see if she's free?'

'It might be an idea.'

Lizzie *was* free and curious to know what was going on, but there was no way Kerry was going to discuss Piers with her again while he was near.

'How long is it since you dined out?' he asked when they went out into the mellow July night.

Kerry stared at him, wondering if she'd heard aright.

'Quite some time,' she told him wryly. 'Why?'

'It just seems ages since we ate after the funeral. Where is the nearest good restaurant?'

If the situation she found herself in had seemed unreal before, being seated opposite Piers in one of the best eateries in the area was taking the strangeness of it into another dimension.

Subdued lighting was throwing into shadow the hollow planes of his face and intensifying the darkness of the mourning clothes they were still wearing. Not the brightest of settings, and yet her spirits were lifting because they were together again. Just the two of them.

When they'd given their order and were waiting to be served, Piers said levelly, 'It's cards-on-the-table time, Kerry.'

She turned her head away, wishing that it didn't have to be. That they might be there just for the purpose of being with each other. But Piers was right. They each had to know where they stood and so she said, 'You first, then. I need to know if you are intending putting in an appearance on the trauma unit on Monday.'

'Yes, I am. We are both adults. I see no need for us to make a big thing of it. We've worked together before.'

'Yes, and look where *that* got us.'

'That was then. This is now. I don't expect that Dad would have any incompetents like Cosgrove working on *his* team for you to molly-coddle.'

She'd known *that* name would come up sooner or later, though he'd said it calmly enough. In the days before he'd left it had been like a red rag to a bull and, fool that she'd been, she'd done nothing to mend matters.

'And what about *your* plans?' he asked tightly. 'Your threat that you would leave Dad's house and find a place of your own? Are you still intending doing that? Obviously I can't stop you if you are determined, but it won't be fair to Rosalie if you do. Whatever our marriage lacks, we are both a hundred per cent wanting to be there for *her*, so let's make the best of it by you both staying where you are. *We* don't need to see much of each other. Just as long as I can see my daughter.'

How could he be so cold and clinical? she thought miserably. And how could he say they wouldn't need to see much of each other when they would be working side by side in a tense emergency environment?

She wasn't to know that he was floundering. Panicking because he was saying all the wrong things. The thought of her taking Rosalie out of his reach was too much to bear. He'd come back with no clear ideas in his mind regarding Kerry and himself. All he'd known had been that he had to see her again. He'd needed to know what was going on in her life. Whether she was still babysitting Cosgrove, or if 'little boy lost' had found himself an even firmer niche in her affairs.

He accepted that he'd been too dictatorial in the past but his hackles still rose when he thought of the incompetent registrar.

'If that's how you feel, we'll stay,' she said stiffly. 'But it's the sufferance thing again, isn't it? You'll put up with me to be near Rosalie.'

'If that is how you prefer to see it…yes,' he said quietly, as relief washed over him.

When the food was served, they ate it mechanically without any further discussion, and Kerry thought, Was that it? Just the bare bones of what the future held? A household held together by a child. It wouldn't be the first time and it wouldn't be the last.

She supposed she should be thankful that *some* good was coming out of what had happened to her father-in-law. Maybe he was looking down on them and thinking that *he* had brought them together again and now it was up to *them*.

A comforting thought if they were both of like mind, but the man sitting opposite had changed. He kept his thoughts to himself these days, with just the odd comment to let her see that the past was still creating a barrier to the future.

As they walked home in the summer dusk there seemed to be lovers all around them. Teenagers at the bus stop, gazing into each other's eyes, unmoving. A couple in their thirties, smart and attractive, getting into an open-topped car with the promise of more to come in their body language, and an elderly pair walking hand in hand towards their bedtime cocoa and the comfort of each other's familiar presence.

Kerry sighed. She could do without the reminders of what *they'd* thrown away. Wrapped in her own thoughts, she stumbled over a tree root and Piers's arm shot out to steady her.

'Are you all right?' he asked in quick concern.

'I'm not sure,' she told him, looking down on to her foot. 'I've twisted my ankle.'

They were almost at the house and, still supporting her, he said, 'Lean on me. We'll be home in a moment and I'll have a look at it.'

'Surely you haven't had *that* much to drink,' Lizzie teased when she saw them.

'I've hurt my ankle—tripped over a tree root,' Kerry told her ruefully as she eased herself into a chair.

'Lucky you've got a doctor on hand, then,' her friend said meaningfully, and Kerry felt the colour start to rise in her cheeks.

'It's nothing serious,' she said hurriedly, looking down at her aching ankle.

'I'll be the judge of that,' Piers said.

'And I'll be on my way now that I know you are in good hands,' Lizzie told her.

She was in 'good hands' all right, Kerry thought as Piers gently examined her foot. She craved his touch. The nearest she'd been to him since he'd come back had been when he'd grabbed her in those first moments of him having discovered that he was a father. But there had been no actual bodily contact and now she was finding that nothing had changed. His touch on her skin was like it had always been, the beginning of desire.

Piers looked up suddenly and she sensed that he'd guessed her thoughts as his hands had become still, his eyes darkening. And *she* was holding her breath.

But it would seem that he was in control even if she wasn't. He may have sensed her reaction to his touch, but he wasn't going to do anything about it. And should she be surprised? He'd already made it clear that he was only accepting her back into his life because of Rosalie. She had a rival in her own daughter.

'It's just a sprain,' he said. 'A pad soaked in witch hazel and a crêpe bandage for support should do the trick. Do you want me to carry you up to bed?'

'No, thanks. I can manage,' she told him with deceptive calm. 'I'm relieved that it's nothing worse. I can't afford to be off my feet with Rosalie to care for and the job.'

'Yes, well, now you've got me around to help with Rosalie and if ever you want to be a stay-at-home parent, it would be no problem. I can easily support the three of us.'

She was getting the message, she thought angrily. Piers wanted the best of both worlds—his daughter where he could see her all the time, with his wife as part of the deal for convenience's sake, but not working with him if he could help it.

He'd said earlier that he wasn't bothered about the arrangement. Yet at the first opportunity he was suggesting that *she* give up the most interesting and rewarding job she'd ever done, and let her A and E nursing skills lie idle.

'There is no way I'm going to give up my job, not as long as Lizzie is around to look after Rosalie while I'm working,' she told him coldly. 'You haven't been back on the scene five minutes and you're out to disrupt the life I've made for myself in your absence. I'm a tried and trusted member of the trauma unit, while *you* have yet to prove yourself.'

'I think I might have already done that,' he told her with equal frostiness, 'as they've offered me the position.'

Determined not to let him gain the upper hand, she flashed back, 'Yes, but they haven't seen you in action yet, have they? Haven't seen what a short fuse you've got. There is no time for personalities to get in the way of the job. Every second counts.'

'Well, thanks for the lecture,' he said dryly. 'I'll bear all of what you've said in mind and if I don't come up to scratch I'm sure you'll be the first one to tell me.'

She would have liked to make a dignified exit instead of hobbling off up the stairs, but if her movements weren't exactly precise, her comments would have left him in no doubt about her determination not to let him crowd her out of health care.

He'd done it again, Piers thought as she disappeared from sight. Said the wrong thing. Made the wrong suggestion. He was normally the most articulate of men. His fluency of speech had got him into trouble a few times as he could always find the right words when others were floundering, but not since he'd come back to be with Kerry. It seemed as if he was incapable of talking coherently about anything, and he knew why. He was being given a second chance and was scared stiff of blowing it.

There'd been a moment when he'd been examining her foot that he'd sensed that Kerry wasn't as immune to him as she was making out. That she hadn't forgotten how at one time they'd only needed to touch each other and passion had been there. It had been one of the reasons why he'd gone off like a rocket when he'd found her in someone else's arms.

He'd known that before Cosgrove he, Piers, had been the only man Kerry had ever slept with. She'd been a virgin when they'd married and at the time he'd revelled in the thought that he would be the first and only one to make love to her.

On the day he'd found her in Cosgrove's arms he'd seen red and accused her of sleeping with him, and she hadn't denied it. Just looked at him as if he'd come from another planet and then slammed out of the staffroom where he'd found them.

It had been his pride that had been hurt more than anything. The thought that she could prefer a drip like that to himself. And now it seemed that he might have been wrong as Cosgrove didn't appear to be anywhere on the scene, but an unexpected pregnancy, rather than a clear conscience, could be the reason for that.

You've buried your father today and taken a step backwards in getting to know your wife again, he told himself sombrely as he checked the doors and windows before going to bed. Nice work.

It was Monday morning and Kerry was not looking forward to what lay ahead. It would be her first day on the unit without Daniel's genial presence and the first time in what seemed like an eternity since she'd worked with Piers.

Having taken leave after her father-in-law's death, she didn't know just how aware the others were about his son joining them, and it went without saying that there would be some curious glances as most of those she worked with had known that she was separated from Daniel's son.

The simplest way to deal with that would be to let them think they were reconciled and his appearance would then be seen as just another new appointment in Accident and Emergency.

Lizzie had arrived as usual at seven-thirty and all that remained was for Piers and herself to get in their cars and proceed to the hospital, but first she had a suggestion to put to him.

As he slid into the driver's seat she bent to speak to him through the open window and hoped that her strong words of the night before might seem less hurtful in the light of day.

'There are going to be some awkward moments

during the coming days, with the two of us working together so soon after your father's death,' she said quietly.

'Yes, possibly there will be,' he agreed levelly. 'But I would have been starting on the unit this morning in any case. It was all arranged.'

Unknown to me, she would have liked to point out, but it was harmony between them that she was seeking, not a further angry exchange of words.

'Yes. I know that,' she agreed. 'But I was thinking it would be less awkward all round and would save a lot of conjecture if we allowed everyone at work to think that we are back together in the real sense. They'll find out that we're living in the same house soon enough, so it shouldn't be hard to persuade them that we're sleeping in the same bed.'

'So you're suggesting that we put on a show.'

Ignoring the irony, she nodded. 'It would be just until you've settled in at the hospital, and Daniel's death and your arrival on the unit so soon after it cease to be a subject of interest to everyone.'

He shrugged and said, 'I don't care a damn what anyone thinks. I'll play *my* part if that's what you want. But are you sure that *you* want us to be all lovey-dovey on the job, making a mockery of the way we really feel? And on *that* subject, children are very susceptible to atmosphere. I think it's time *you* thawed out, for Rosalie's sake.'

'Do you really?' she sparked back. 'So as usual I'm the one at fault. We'll discuss *that* another time if it's all the same to you.' And going across to her own vehicle, she left him to lead the way to the city centre.

*   *   *

So Kerry wanted people to think they slept in the same bed, Piers was thinking grimly as he wove his way through the traffic with her close behind. He couldn't think of anything he would like more than that, but they were a long way from that being the truth, and instead she was suggesting they put on an act to take the attention of others off them.

He had always thought her beautiful and, now in motherhood she was even more desirable, but it wouldn't be easy to pretend that all was well with their marriage when it wasn't. Deceit didn't come easily to him and he deplored it in others. Yet in spite of what he'd said earlier, neither did he want them to be the object of gossip, so he supposed he was going to go along with the idea for the time being.

They'd been the kind of couple that people had looked at twice in the days before they'd separated. Kerry the tranquil, blonde nurse and Piers the surgeon with hair as dark as anthracite, eyes full of purpose and a vibrancy about him that had made other men seem insignificant, Danny Cosgrove in particular.

Though it had turned out that the guy hadn't been all that weak. He'd been smart enough to get Kerry fussing round him with his woebegone expression always on view and had come out on top. In how many ways *he* might never know. But at least the child who had him entranced wasn't Cosgrove's. He'd been spared that humiliation.

Following him along the London roads, Kerry was beginning to wonder if having Piers back in her life was worth the doubts and uncertainties that his return had brought with it.

While he'd been away she had achieved a sort of numb contentment, which though it could hardly be called living had got her through the days. But now it was like battling with an open wound, raw and painful.

The introductions were over. The night shift had gone and the day team were getting ready to face another day without the man who'd been at the centre of their excellence.

That his son had been appointed to work alongside them so soon after his father's death was a strange trick of fate...and Kerry, who'd been one of them for quite some time now, was surprising them all by appearing to be on good terms with her husband.

But the city was out there, ready to remind them that there were more important matters to attend to than their own affairs and those of other members of the team.

When the paramedics came hurrying in with those they'd been called out to, or the helicopter came whirring onto the rooftop with its cargo plucked off the ground, they became as one.

A motorcyclist who'd hit the side of a bus was the first of the day shift's problems and just one look at him was enough to tell them they had to act fast. There was a gaping wound in the back of his neck that was very near the jugular vein lying at the base of the skull.

His helmet had protected his head above it, but it looked as if a metal spike of some kind, probably from his motorcycle as it had disintegrated, had penetrated the neck below it.

'There could be damage to the heart and brain besides the gaping hole in the neck,' Piers said as the injured biker was lifted carefully onto the table. 'We need to check them out first. Hopefully the crash helmet will have saved his head from serious injury, but it doesn't always follow.'

Tom Marsden, a surgeon who had been one of the first to be approached by Daniel when he'd been forming the unit, nodded his agreement and Kerry, gowned, scrubbed up and ready to act upon every requirement of the two surgeons, was aware of her heartbeat pounding in her ears as one of the radiologists on the team performed the necessary X-rays.

Incredibly, they showed there was no damage to the heart, and the helmet *had* prevented brain damage, but the lungs had collapsed and if there was still fluid trapped in them they would have to be drained before being reinflated.

As the two surgeons battled to stem the blood and close the neck wound, it was like old times. It was as if it was only yesterday that she and Piers had been doing this sort of thing together. Sharing in the satisfaction of a life saved, and accepting it bleakly when it wasn't. She'd been longing to work with him again, yet at the same time dreading it.

Watching him doing the job that meant so much to him with the cool competence that was so much Piers Jefferson, she wondered if somewhere Daniel was smiling his approval because *some* of his plotting had paid off.

But this was the easy part, she thought. Emergency

surgery was to Piers what water was to a duck. It was in the damaged remains of their marriage that the problem lay.

'Right, Kerry,' he was saying, with hand outstretched across the table, and she passed him the instrument required.

Tom said, 'I can see that the two of you have worked together before. You read each other's minds, anticipate each other's needs.'

'I wish!' Piers murmured dryly for her ears only from behind his mask.

'How much longer?' the anaesthetist asked from the top end of the operating table.

As Kerry eyed Piers stonily he said, 'We're almost done.'

'What do you think his chances are?' the other man asked.

'As good as we can possibly give him. We managed to close the wound without any damage to the jugular vein, which was our main concern. The lungs have been cleared and reinflated and with efficient nursing care he should make a good recovery, though it might take some time.'

As they prepared to transfer the injured biker to Intensive Care a young nurse came in to say that the patient's mother was waiting outside, desperate for news of her son.

'I'll speak to her as soon as I've cleaned up,' Piers told her, adding to Kerry, who was close by, 'I see you haven't lost the touch where the job is concerned.'

'Meaning?'

'Meaning nothing. I was merely commenting, that's all.'

'Throwing me a crumb more like it.'

He shrugged. 'See it how you will.' And without further comment he went to speak to the anxious woman out in the corridor.

As Kerry listened from a distance she couldn't hear what he was saying, but his voice was calm and reassuring and she thought that he had a kind word for everyone except her.

When he found her having a quick coffee later in the staff restaurant he came across, gave her a hug, and said breezily, 'Just like old times, wasn't it, sweetheart?'

One of the radiologists who'd helped save the life of the injured motorcyclist was seated nearby, along with a junior doctor, so Kerry guessed that the comment was for their benefit and in keeping with her suggestion earlier.

She was wishing now that she'd never made it. A display of false affection on Piers's part was going to be hard to stomach and there was a gleam in his eye that said he guessed as much.

'Yes, it is,' she said serenely, adding in an undertone, 'Don't overdo it.'

He laughed and went on his way, while she flashed an enigmatic smile in the direction of the listeners.

After that there was little time to think about anything other than the continued arrival of the sick and injured by ambulance or helicopter.

Amongst them was a teenager with a shattered leg. He'd been standing at a bus stop when a woman

driver had lost control of her car and careered onto
the pavement, hitting him on the leg.

The fractures were serious and the paramedics who
brought him in were concerned in case blood wasn't
circulating to his toes, which could result in him losing the limb.

The orthopaedic surgeon on the team took over immediately and was able to reassure them that there
were no circulation problems so far, but that extensive
surgery was needed urgently to repair the shattered
bones and prevent blood loss to the toes.

The lad was in a lot of pain and concerned that he
wouldn't be able to play football again.

'We can't guarantee that you'll play football in the
near future, but with a bit of luck you'll walk,' she
heard Piers tell him. 'Once we've pinned you together
again.'

He turned to one of the paramedics who were hov-
ering nearby. 'What happened to the woman in the
car? Is she next on our list?'

The man shook his head. 'No. It was a heart attack.
She's gone straight into Coronary Care.'

'She nearly killed me!' the lad sobbed.

'Yes, but she wouldn't have known anything about
it,' Kerry told him gently as they waited for the an-
aesthetic to kick in. 'If a motorist is taken ill at the
wheel, a very dangerous situation develops if they're
not well enough to stop the car.'

'This kid has been hurt really badly,' Piers said
sombrely a little later as he and the orthopaedic surgeon repaired the shattered leg. 'He was in the wrong
place at the wrong time, poor lad, with disastrous results.'

As Kerry listened she thought that was what had happened to her. For a brief weak moment she had accepted the comfort of another man's arms because those of the man she loved had never been there for her at that time.

In those few seconds Piers had found her and the discovery had pushed him too far. The results had been disastrous, like they'd been for the boy on the table, though the hurts that followed had been mental rather than physical.

CHAPTER THREE

Piers was first home. Kerry had stopped off to buy a take-away and when Lizzie opened the door to him his first words were, 'Is Rosalie asleep?'

She smiled.

'Yes. We *do* have our routine, you know.'

He sighed.

'Mmm. I suppose so, but so do she and I, and bath time is one of the highlights of the day.'

'So after a hard day glued to the operating table you're still wanting time with your daughter. That must be how Kerry has often felt,' Lizzie pointed out, 'but a working parent has to make choices and they also have to bring in the cash.'

'All right, I'm getting the message,' he told her, 'but there would have been no need for any of this if she'd listened to reason in the first place.'

It was at that moment Kerry arrived with the food. She heard the last part of what he was saying and it wiped out the good feeling that the day had brought.

Lizzie saw her face twist and said, 'Piers is disappointed that the main attraction is in the land of nod. I was just about to tell him that you should both take advantage of it and have a quiet meal together. And while you do that I'll be on my way. See you both tomorrow.'

'So how did you think the day went?' he asked as they ate.

51

'I thought it went extremely well,' she told him flatly. 'It was great to see you in action again, until I heard you criticising me to Lizzie. You really are the most self-righteous and unforgiving man I've ever met.'

'So you don't think I apportion any blame to myself for what went wrong between us? And when it comes to forgiveness, what about the daughter I didn't know I had? I've accepted that, haven't I?'

Kerry pushed her plate away and got to her feet.

'I'm going to bed. I'm not prepared to keep going over the same old ground…and you won't be lonely while you've got your ego for company.'

'Watching that husband of yours at work today was like seeing Daniel all over again,' one of the anaethetists had said to her as they'd been peeling off their gowns at the end of the day. 'It must have given you a real lift, working with him.'

'Yes, it did,' she'd said softly. 'It was like old times. We worked together when we were first married and I'd forgotten what a good feeling it was.'

As she lay sleepless against the pillows Kerry thought that she'd also forgotten for a short time that there was a different agenda to their marriage now. They'd joined the ever-increasing number of couples who gave up at the first sign of strife and she wasn't proud of it.

But there were two of them in the marriage. If ever they were to get back together it would have to be with forgiveness on both sides. Not herself as the one building bridges and Piers rubbing it in at every opportunity that he was the wronged party, when he hadn't been.

In the middle of the night she went downstairs to get a drink and something to make her sleep, and was amazed to see the door of his room wide open and the bed not slept in.

Surely Piers hadn't gone again after what she'd said earlier, she thought frantically. She wouldn't be able to bear it if he had. Crossing swiftly to the wardrobe, she saw his clothes still hanging there, but it didn't alter the fact that the room was empty.

He was nowhere to be seen in the downstairs rooms and she felt sick. Why couldn't they behave kindly to each other? she thought raggedly. If the love had gone they could at least be polite.

As she went to the fridge she saw him, silhouetted against the moonlit skyline at the bottom of the garden, and forgetting what had gone before she hurried out to him.

'I thought you'd gone again,' she told him when she appeared beside him.

'And would it have mattered if I had?'

'Yes.'

'Why? I'm a pain in the neck most of the time, aren't I?'

'You're also my husband and Rosalie's father.'

'But we're not exactly playing at happy families, are we?'

His glance went to the globes of her breasts, jutting beneath a flimsy nightdress, and the smooth white stem of her neck. Desire was wiping out everything except longing.

Kerry saw the look in his eyes and felt her body responding.

'What?' she questioned.

'You're still the most beautiful woman I've ever seen...and the most unapproachable.'

'I don't recall you trying to approach me,' she murmured.

'Well, maybe I should. It's a long time since I saw the mole on your thigh and the tattoo on your shoulder.'

There was silence for a moment, then she said slowly, 'I haven't got a tattoo.'

He laughed. 'It must have been some other woman I bedded, but you *have* got the mole, haven't you?'

'So you've slept with other women?' she said slowly.

'It was a joke.'

'Am I supposed to believe that?'

'It's up to you. I had to make the same decision about you and Cosgrove and it's not easy to sort out the truth from the not so true.'

She sighed. Incredibly, just a moment ago, they'd been ready to make love. But his flippancy about something so vital to them finding any degree of understanding had put the blight on it.

'I'm going back to bed,' she told him. '*On my own.* And if you've any sense you'll do the same, or you'll be nodding off at the operating table tomorrow.'

Kerry didn't give him time to reply. She went back inside, picked up her drink off the kitchen table and went quickly up the stairs. After a quick peep at Rosalie she went into her room and closed the door behind her with a decisive click.

It was some minutes before Piers followed her. She heard him go into the nursery as he did each night before going to his solitary bed and thought that they were so near, yet so far from being the kind of family she wanted them to be. Would she ever understand him? was her last thought before sleep came.

He hadn't slept with any woman since her, Piers had thought bleakly when, moving wraithlike and determined amongst the plants and shrubs, Kerry had made her way back to the house. Surely she knew him better than that.

He was angry to think she'd taken him up on a silly joke and believed it. Yet he'd been ready to think the same thing of her, hadn't he? It did him no credit that he should see it from a different angle when it came to himself.

When he came out of the nursery it registered with him that her door was well and truly closed against him and he found himself smiling. She usually kept it ajar so that she would hear Rosalie if she awoke, but not tonight. The closed door said that *he* could listen out for her, but, then, he did in any case. She had only to turn over and he was half out of bed. If his love for Kerry had turned out to be a poor thing, the way he felt about his daughter had no flaws in it. When she came toddling towards him with arms outstretched he was putty in her tiny hands.

In the days that followed those moments in the moonlit garden there was a degree of calm between them. The demands of daily living were enough to occupy them. Caring for Rosalie, their jobs and the never-ending aftermath of his father's death to sort out for Piers.

But it didn't stop them from being achingly aware of each other's every glance, every action. It was like being attracted to someone for the first time, Kerry thought. They were involved in the process of desperately wanting to see into the mind of someone else, but not wanting to admit it.

Each day as it came was a mixture of challenge and uncertainty. Waiting to see what the other person would say. How they would act, and hoping that it would be how one wanted them to be. Only in their case they'd already been there and done that and were on the second time round.

If Piers felt the same way he didn't show it, and she thought again that the days were long gone when *he* had been honest and open in all his dealings with *her*.

The surprise at Piers's arrival on the trauma team had now died down. There had been some curiosity at first as to what the extent of his abilities were as the son of Daniel Jefferson, but it hadn't taken long for the other surgeons, anaesthetists and radiologists to decide that it was like father, like son. He was good.

When it came to getting to know him, however, it wasn't easy. He wasn't the type one could get chummy with. Though one or two of the women wouldn't have minded the chance. They observed that Jefferson was affectionate towards his wife when they were together on the unit, but they didn't always sit together at break times and sometimes she looked as if she would rather he didn't fuss over her.

But up there amongst the rooftops there was little time for anything other than attending to the sick and injured who came through their doors. The private lives of their colleagues were just that and no one interfered.

On a Monday morning in early August a teenager was brought in from a street fight. He'd been part of a gang rampaging around one of the shopping malls, but any bravado he might have possessed had disappeared as he was unloaded from the helicopter onto the operating table with multiple injuries.

As Piers and Tom bent over him he whimpered, 'Is this where the doc who was knocked down worked?'

Watching from the other side of the table, Kerry saw Piers's dark brows rise.

'It might be,' he said calmly, continuing his examination of the patient. 'Why do you ask?'

'The police have been round to see me.'

'And why would that be?' he murmured, telling Kerry in an aside, 'Fetch the radiologist. This laddie could have a pelvic fracture. There's blood coming from the rectum.'

So you're not going to let me die because they think I was one of those that tripped him up?' he whined.

Kerry saw anger bleach her husband's face.

'And were you?'

'Might have been.'

'No. I am not going to let you die if I can help it,' he said with steely control. 'We're not all mindless morons. But you won't be making a nuisance of yourself on the streets of the city for some time to come with what others like yourself have done to you.'

He was incredible, Kerry thought. Still with a great grief inside him he was the surgeon, the lifesaver first and foremost, and that was how his father would have wanted him to be.

When the lad had been dealt with Piers told the others, 'I need some air.' And when his wife followed close on his heels there were sympathetic glances all round.

Kerry found him gazing sombrely over the rooftops in a small garden area beside the helipad.

'I could have throttled him,' he choked. 'Thereby doing both myself and the NHS a favour.'

'The police will deal with him,' she said softly, taking his hand in hers. 'The foolish kid has just more or less admitted he was involved. He wouldn't have been so scared at being brought here otherwise. That sort of mind expects the same kind of treatment that it metes out to others.'

Piers nodded and as she watched the tension begin to leave his expression he said, 'Yes, I suppose you're right. But what a twist of fate that young lout being brought to me of all people to be treated.'

'He might have learned something today,' she said gently

'Such as?'

'That we don't all want an eye for an eye.'

For the rest of the day Piers shut out the distressing conversation with the injured youth and concentrated on those moments with Kerry. There had been genuine concern on her part and it had melted some of the ice around his heart.

That evening, after settling Rosalie in her cot, he

went to seek her out with the intention of trying to bring back the feeling of togetherness that they'd experienced in the rooftop garden.

He'd left her in the kitchen, clearing up, but as he went down the stairs Piers was aware that stillness had fallen upon the house. There was no clatter of pots and pans or cupboard doors opening and shutting, and his step quickened.

When he reached the kitchen door he found her standing motionless at the sink with warm suds almost up to her elbows. She was gazing out over the garden, her thoughts far away, but when she heard his footsteps behind her she turned to face him.

'What's wrong?' he asked.

'Nothing,' she said quickly. 'I was just daydreaming. Back in the past for a few moments.'

'Really?' he commented dryly. 'Which part of the past would that be? The good or the bad? It's obvious that Cosgrove isn't around, so do I take it that he ended up surplus to requirements?'

He was praying that she would say 'yes' and at the same time was thinking that this wasn't what he'd been planning when he'd come downstairs.

'You can't forget Danny, can you?' she said, as if sudden weariness had fallen upon her. 'You know very well that he meant nothing to me. How do I know that you didn't use him as an excuse to get rid of me?'

'What?' he cried. 'I'll pretend I didn't hear that. You know very well I would never do anything so despicable. I adored you.'

'And I adored you, but look where it got us.'

'I would hope that we've grown up a bit since then.'

'I certainly have,' Kerry told him wryly. 'It's amazing how becoming a parent changes one's outlook. Take you, for instance. You would spend every moment of the day with Rosalie if you could, wouldn't you?'

He nodded. 'Yes, I would, but, then, I have a lot of time to make up with her.'

'I *do* know that,' she told him, 'and we are both equally to blame for it.'

At that moment a thud from upstairs had them both looking upwards, and Kerry said, 'It would seem that someone is still awake and dropping things out of her cot.'

'So let's go and investigate,' Piers said immediately, and she decided he'd had enough of grim reminiscences.

Rosalie *was* still awake. She was smiling at them over the bars of the cot and all the toys that she usually slept with were on the floor.

'Daddy,' she said suddenly as Piers bent to pick them up, and he became still.

'Did you hear what she said?' he breathed. 'The first full word she's said and it was "Daddy".'

'So does that make you feel any better?' Kerry asked with a smile. 'If I can't say the right thing it would seem that Rosalie doesn't suffer from the same failing.'

'Are you asking if it makes up for all the time she and I were apart?' he questioned.

'Yes.'

'Hmm. It does in part.'

'Good,' she said evenly, and with a strong feeling of being the odd one out she left them together and went for a leisurely soak in the hope that it would soothe her frazzled nerves.

When she surfaced from the bathroom some time later the house was quiet. Rosalie was asleep and there was no sign of Piers. Maybe he, too, had felt the need to unwind she thought and had gone for a drink in one of the many bars in the area.

There was a scribbled note on the kitchen table that said merely, 'Don't wait up for me.' And she thought, *I won't!* It was clear that now his evenings were not as occupied with his father's affairs, he didn't want her company. That after a long hard day at the hospital he needed to get away from her.

Working together on the unit was something he couldn't avoid, but there was nothing to say that he had to stay with her in the evenings once his daughter was asleep.

Piers had always had plenty of pent-up energy and if he wanted to use it for some socialising it was his affair. As for herself she was exhausted, and once her head touched the pillow she was asleep in minutes. But it wasn't to last.

She woke up a couple of hours later to the sound of a car engine cutting out on the drive down below, and when she gazed sleepily at the bedside clock it showed one o'clock in the morning.

Minutes later she heard Piers mounting the stairs, was aware of him going into Rosalie's room, then his bedroom door clicked shut and she turned over and went back to sleep, relieved to know that, wherever he'd been, he was back.

Kerry didn't open her eyes again until the smell of coffee and bacon grilling brought her back to consciousness. That and the fact that Rosalie's cot was empty indicated that she was going to be last up. Sure enough, when she went downstairs Piers was at the cooker, looking scrubbed, and fresh after his late night, and Rosalie was spooning up her breakfast cereal with hungry concentration.

When Kerry appeared in the doorway he lifted his head and, with his cool, dark gaze taking in the shadows under her eyes and the tousled blonde mop, said, 'You look as if you've had a restless night.'

'Not at all,' she fibbed. 'I've slept like a log.' *And feel like one.*

'You're sure I didn't disturb you when I came in?'

Was he giving her an opening to ask where he'd been? she wondered. If he was, she wasn't going to give him the satisfaction of knowing she was curious.

'No. I didn't hear a thing,' she told him as she poured herself some juice, and seemingly with no further comments to make he turned back to what was happening under the grill.

That day on the unit it seemed as if all London was accident prone. The first patient to be lifted out of the helicopter was a window cleaner who had fallen off a high ladder while working outside some apartments.

He had head and back injuries and was strapped to a spinal board to avoid any further damage in that area. X-rays of the skull taken from different angles showed evidence of an open fracture where bone fragments had been displaced inwardly, and a neurologist, with Piers working alongside, was going to have to remove the fragments and repair the damaged tissue.

Surgery on injured vertebrae of the spine resulting from the fall would take place once the man had come through the first operation and in that instance X-rays showed that fortunately it would be a case of bone realignment rather than disposing of shattered fragments.

Both Kerry and Piers knew there was always a risk of serious infections such as meningitis after skull surgery and once the patient was transferred to the ward, antibiotics would be given as a preventative.

'My head!' he'd kept moaning. 'It hurts.'

'Yes, we know it does,' Piers told him gravely. 'Just hang on in there. We're going to do something about it as fast as we can.'

At that moment another accident victim was brought in, this time an elderly lady who had fallen in a supermarket and had a suspected fracture of the hip.

She was bewildered at being picked up and deposited on the roof in the middle of her weekly shop and agitated because there would be no one to feed her cat if she wasn't allowed home.

A junior nurse was sent to phone a neighbour to explain what had happened and ask her to look after the precious pet, and once that was done the patient began to calm down.

'Someone had spilt a bottle of orange squash and I slipped on it,' she said as she waited to be X-rayed.

She was sounding less anxious now that she was more comfortable and arrangements had been made for her cat, almost as if she was enjoying the attention. Kerry thought that even a visit to hospital was an exciting event to those who had little going on in their lives. It was to be hoped that the suspected hip fracture would be repairable as it wasn't always the case. But the elderly accident victim was in the right place for the best possible treatment.

'A cleaner was on her way with a mop and bucket,' she told Kerry, 'but it was too late. I was on the floor by then.' As Kerry smiled in sympathy she went on to say, 'If I have to have an operation I don't want one of those anaesthetics where they put you to sleep. I want an epidurex, even if I have to listen to them sawing.'

'I think that you mean an epidural,' Kerry said, turning away to hide a smile, 'and the doctors *will* bear that in mind.'

And so it went on, with every available theatre in use and all the staff fully occupied.

There was to be no epidural for the window cleaner during surgery, his injuries were too severe.

As Kerry anticipated the requirements of the two surgeons with the swift precision that came from years in Theatre, she was wishing that the other part of her life with Piers was as rewarding as this. Not only did they help to heal and save, they met all kinds of people, often in the worst physical condition they'd ever been in, and as they fought to survive it was humbling to be able to offer their skills.

She looked up and caught Piers watching her and thought that nothing was going to make her give up this job. He'd had a nerve to even suggest it.

*   *   *

'I was wondering where you'd got to,' he said that night when he met her at the door with Rosalie pink and perfect in her pyjamas. 'I thought you were just behind me in the traffic. Is everything all right?'

'Yes, now it is. I *should* have been behind you,' she told him, 'but there was a panic while we were counting and sterilising the instruments at the end of the day.'

'Why?' he asked, immediately tuned in.

'A pair of scissors was missing.'

'And?'

'We found them eventually, but it took time.'

'I suppose you thought they'd been left inside a patient.'

'It *has* happened before.' She managed a tired smile. 'But not with *you* on the job. It was one of the nurses who wasn't concentrating as she should have been.'

He was frowning. 'Which one?'

'Don't ask me,' she said evasively, remembering how he'd been with Danny Cosgrove. 'We're all only human, you know, Piers. None of us are perfect, including you. Though you might think you are. The girl we're talking about has quite a few family problems.'

'Huh! Who hasn't?' he parried meaningfully. 'But when we are responsible for the lives of others we have to put our own problems in a separate compartment. The person in question will be adding to her worries in a big way if she doesn't keep her mind on the job.'

'I know,' she agreed wearily, 'but can we, please, forget it?'

She wanted a shower, a glass of wine and some food in that order.

'You're exhausted,' he said, reading her mind. 'I've started preparing the meal. It won't be long before we eat. Shall I pour you a drink.'

Kerry shook her head. 'I'm going to have a shower first, but before that I want a kiss from my daughter, who again doesn't look very tired.'

'Yes, young miss is not yet ready for sleep,' he agreed, smiling down at Rosalie's dark curls. 'I was home reasonably early so Lizzie was able to make a quick get-away and I thought that for once Rosalie could stay up to see her mum.'

Kerry felt tears prick. On the face of it they were an ordinary loving family, but underneath there were bridges to be rebuilt, truths to be established, and how long was that going to take?

'I've got two tickets for a show in the West End,' Piers said without looking up as they cleared away after the meal. 'One of the radiologists was trying to unload them. Something has cropped up to stop her and her partner from going. They're for Saturday night and I thought that maybe Lizzie would babysit if we asked her. That is, if you would like to go.'

'Yes, I would,' she told him, trying to hide her surprise.

So far all their home-based activities had been around Rosalie. The feeling that she, Kerry, was just part of the package had been strong, but maybe she'd been wrong. Maybe the spark was still there, and she supposed that even if it wasn't, the two of them going out to a show wasn't to be sneezed at.

*   *   *

Every time she thought about Saturday night Kerry found herself smiling. It was like having a date, but not with a handsome stranger. The man in question was her husband. But that *was* the only difference, as they didn't come any more spellbinding to look upon and be with than Piers Jefferson.

That other life, when she'd romanced with him, slept with him, adored him, seemed far, far away, and all because what could only be described as lack of trust had turned it into a bitter battle of wills, but at least they were living in each other's proximity once more.

Kerry felt butterflies in her stomach, along with a thrill of anticipation, as she zipped herself into a dress that had been Piers's favourite once. When he'd gone it had been put out of sight with all the other things that had reminded her of him, but she felt that maybe tonight it might come into its own.

Of soft, jasmine silk with a low neckline, tight bodice and a fluted skirt, it made a statement against the fair cap of her hair, and for the first time in weeks she felt like her own person, rather than Rosalie's mother or Piers Jefferson's estranged wife.

He didn't comment when she appeared but there was a look in his eyes that told her he hadn't forgotten the dress and might be getting the message. Yet *would* he? And if he did, unless he could tell her that he trusted her it didn't matter how *she* looked or how *he* felt.

Piers was ready first and when he came to ask if she was ready to go he found her in front of the mirror, trying to fasten a heavy gold necklace.

'Here, let me,' he said.

When he'd fastened it he stood observing her re-flection with his hands resting on her shoulders. Kerry felt herself tensing. His touch was light, yet it felt as if it was burning her skin, and there was a look in his eyes that she hadn't seen in a long time.

It made her think that if she had a choice she would suggest they shut the bedroom door and forget about the theatre. But Lizzie had just arrived and was wait-ing for them to depart and she couldn't think of a sensible reason why they shouldn't go.

So she brought them back to earth by asking the time-honoured question of those about to hit the town. 'Have you got the tickets?'

Piers removed his hands from her shoulders. 'Yes,' he said flatly. 'I've got the tickets. Shall we go?'

It was the first night of a new show and there was a buzz in the air as they took their seats.

'I've arranged a meal at a new restaurant that is highly recommended for afterwards,' Piers had said as they'd driven towards the theatre. 'So it's all new tonight. New show, new restaurant, and a...'

He didn't finish the sentence and Kerry hoped that he'd been about to say 'new beginning'. But if that *had* been the case, why hadn't he said it?

At the first interval she sat back in her seat and looked around her. She couldn't remember the last time she'd been out socially like this and to be there with Piers of all people was incredible.

As if reading her thoughts, he reached over and took her hand in his. It was her left hand and, gazing down on to her wedding ring, he said, 'I was surprised to see it still on your finger when I came back.'

'And what would you have done if it hadn't been?'

'The question didn't arise,' he said smoothly.

'I saw no reason to take it off. I wasn't going anywhere. I was pregnant, remember.'

'Yes, I haven't forgotten. I hope you realise that I would never have gone if I'd known.'

The smoothness had been replaced by a harsh sort of intensity and, meeting his dark gaze, she told him, 'And I would never have let you stay...not from a sense of duty. But as you've just said, it was a question that didn't arise, and we're going to spoil the evening if we start harking back to the past, Piers. It's the present that matters...and the future.'

'So do you think we have a future?'

'I don't know. Rosalie needs a father.'

'Yes, but do you need a husband?'

'Maybe. If you know of one who would be prepared to trust me.'

She watched his lips part and wondered what was coming next. But the moment was about to shatter. The smooth voice of management was coming over the public address system and it had them rigid in their seats.

CHAPTER FOUR

'IF MR and Mrs Piers Jefferson are in the theatre, will they please phone their home urgently,' it was saying, and they observed each other in disbelief.

'That's us!' Piers said quietly. 'Whatever can be wrong?'

'Rosalie!' Kerry whispered.

By now they were hurrying up the centre aisle and once they were out of the auditorium Piers switched on his mobile phone and rang the house.

It was answered immediately and as he listened she watched the changing expressions cross his face. First came relief, then concern, followed by tight-lipped purpose.

'What?' she cried. 'What's wrong?'

'That was Lizzie,' he said. 'Rosalie is fine. All is well back at the house. It's us. We've been called in by the hospital. There's been an explosion at a block of flats with lots of casualties. All accident and emergency departments have been alerted and all available staff are being called in. Lizzie says not to worry. She'll stay with Rosalie for as long as it takes. Shall we go?'

She nodded. Of course they would go, and with all speed. That was what they'd been trained for, but why did it have to be tonight?

* * *

70

As dawn broke the team was still operating, using every ounce of skill along with the latest techniques to try and save the lives of the occupants of the apartment building. Fortunately there were no children amongst the injured. It had been a complex occupied almost entirely by business people.

The explosion was thought to have been caused by a ruptured gas main, although there was no actual gas in the building. But the mains were close by and were being investigated by the authorities even as rescuers lifted the injured from the rubble.

A man in his thirties in a smart pinstriped suit now covered in blood and grime was one of the first casualties to be brought in. He was in deep shock, holding on tightly to what was left of a briefcase. When his jacket had been cut away they found that the hand clutching just the leather handle belonged to an arm that was almost severed.

It would need immediate microsurgery to rejoin the nerves and vessels if the limb was to be saved, as the longer they remained in that state the less chance there would be of them knitting together again.

The injured man's fiancée had arrived and was weeping uncontrollably in one of the waiting rooms. Kerry and one of the junior nurses went to speak to her before scrubbing up and were told between sobs that the couple had intended to get married the following day.

'I'm so sorry,' Kerry told her. 'You're going to have to fix another date I'm afraid. Your fiancé almost lost an arm in the explosion.'

'I don't care about the wedding,' the young woman sobbed. 'Just as long as Miles doesn't die.'

'Mr Jefferson will come and have a word with you

before the operation,' Kerry told her, and thought that it might be some time before the man in the pinstriped suit was fit enough to face a wedding.

The helicopter rotors whirred above them for the last time at seven o'clock, just as Miles was coming out of surgery, and Piers said, 'Go home, Kerry. Lizzie will be wondering where we've got to. I'm going to have another chat with Ria, Miles's fiancée. She's still huddled out there waiting for news, and at this moment the best I can tell her is we've done all we can to save his arm. She hasn't been in touch with anyone from Miles's family. Says there's no one to tell, which seems a bit odd, but not everyone has a caring family in the background, I suppose.'

'No, indeed,' she agreed, with the thought uppermost that they weren't too high on that list themselves. Her parents had died when she was young. She'd been brought up by an aunt. Piers's mother had died while he'd been in his teens and Daniel's death, though much more recent, had been just as final. As for their own little family set-up, it remained to be seen what was going to happen to that.

'We didn't have to go to the theatre to find drama, did we?' he remarked dryly. 'Though I'd rather have seen it from a seat in the circle. Also, so much for the table for two at Allesandro's. But there will be a few people in Intensive Care who won't be sorry we missed our gastronomic delights.'

The rest of the weekend went all too quickly with no follow-up to the conversation they'd been having in the theatre. For one thing they were both tired after the long, stressful night, and the moment that Rosalie was asleep on Sunday evening her parents followed suit, each to their separate rooms and their separate thoughts.

Lying back against the pillows, Piers was thinking wryly that if anyone ever asked if they'd spent the night together since he'd come back he would be able to say yes in truthful irony. But it hadn't been between the sheets in each other's arms unfortunately. They'd had company—the staff of a trauma unit— and for once he wished it far away.

Kerry's thoughts were travelling along different lines. Whatever their lives lacked they had two things to be thankful for, she was telling herself drowsily. Their daughter and the privilege of working together in one of the most rewarding jobs that anyone could wish for, and as sleep slid over her she vowed to try not to wish for more.

On Monday night Piers announced, 'I'm going round to the Sangsters' tonight. Ian wants to discuss Dad's will with me. He's mentioned it a few times and I've kept putting him off. It seems so final when one has to start talking about money. It will feel like the closing of one chapter of my life and the opening of another...without him.'

Kerry was observing him in surprise. His father's estate hadn't been discussed between them. Piers had never mentioned it and because of that neither had she, deciding that it was not for her to ask questions. What he wanted her to know he would tell her. But she was amazed to hear that he still hadn't seen his father's will. That he'd been putting the moment off.

It wasn't in keeping with the way Piers usually did things.

He was a more decisive sort of person than she was. Quick to act, as she knew to her cost, and impatient with ditherers. But not in this instance, it would seem, and she thought sadly that his hurt must go very deep if he couldn't face up to the reading of Daniel's will.

When he came back from the solicitor's house he had a closed look about him and she asked, 'Is everything all right?'

'Yes,' he said, and went into the study, closing the door behind him.

Kerry frowned. She knew the man too well to believe that there wasn't a problem. But what could be wrong? Daniel had been a wealthy man. And that wealth would now belong to Piers. So why was he looking as if a carrot had been dangled in front of him and then taken away?

As the evening drew to its close he was still in the study and she decided that if he wasn't going to tell her what was wrong, she wasn't going to ask, and on that decision she went to bed.

She had her answer the following day in a phone call from Ian Sangster to the unit.

'I presume that Piers will have told you that your father-in-law left you a very sizeable amount of money and set up a trust fund for his granddaughter,' the elderly solicitor said. 'Obviously I don't want to discuss details over the phone, but if you will make an appointment to see me at my office, I will explain exactly what is involved.'

When he'd gone off the line Kerry shook her head in disbelief. So this was what was bugging Piers, she thought miserably. He didn't agree with what his father had done. *She* was amazed and deeply touched by it.

Daniel had made sure that she was provided for in the event of Piers and herself never becoming reconciled, and for some reason his son wasn't happy about the arrangement. But why? Unless he, Piers, thought she wasn't entitled to it.

Did he think she'd wheedled round his father during his absence with an eye to the main chance or something of the sort? It was insulting if he did and only went to show that they were further off reaching any degree of understanding than she'd thought.

When she went back into Theatre Piers's glance was upon her and she knew he was curious about the call. Or, then again, maybe he wasn't. He would know that Ian Sangster would have to get in touch with her, but if there *were* any questions in the eyes meeting hers he wouldn't have to wait long. The first chance she got she was going to face him and demand to know what the problem was. Was it the money? Or did something deeper lie behind his aloofness?

The opportunity came in the late morning when the team stopped for a break between patients. She collared him in the staffroom and said quietly, 'Have you got a moment?'

He followed her as she led the way to the same rooftop garden where she'd gone to him after he'd treated the youth who'd been involved in the attack on his father.

'That was Ian Sangster on the phone,' she said.

'So he's told you the good news, then?'

'What? That your father has left Rosalie and I provided for? It wasn't of my doing, Piers. I knew nothing about it.'

He shrugged and she wanted to reach out and shake him, get through to what lay beneath, but he was turning to go as if the moment was of little importance. Her patience was running out.

'It's because you don't want me to be independent of you, isn't it?' she cried. 'You'd rather it was you in control and me toeing the line. But your father in his goodness has made me financially independent and you don't like it. If it's going to make you like this I won't take the money. Will *that* suit you? And, Piers, you can take your pique out on me as much as you like, but I hope you don't begrudge our daughter the trust fund that your father has set up in her name.'

A dull red flush was rising on his neck and she knew *that* had got to him if nothing else had. Where *she* was the thorn in his side, their daughter was his Achilles heel, where he was most vulnerable.

'I begrudge neither of you anything,' he said stiffly. 'What my father has left you will make little impact on my inheritance.'

'So what's the problem, for goodness' sake? Why are you treating me like this?' she cried. 'Daniel's wish was to unite us, not drive us further apart.'

'Yes, maybe, but in the scheme of things that he set up he reckoned on being alive to see the results, not make them harder to accomplish.'

'I don't understand what you mean,' she said wearily.

'Think about it,' he replied, adding as the noise of the helicopter approaching broke into the moment, 'It would seem that we are needed.' And without any further enlightenment he pointed himself towards it.

Couldn't she see, Piers thought grimly as he drove home that night, that he was dreading that now his father had made her financially independent Kerry would do what she'd threatened to do before, take Rosalie and find a place of their own?

If it had been said out of bravado then, it needn't be like that now. Daniel had given her the chance of a life of her own and freedom from himself if she wanted it, and he was uneasy, asking himself all the time what he had ever done to make her want to stay with him.

When she'd got over her surprise, would the same thing occur to her? That she could have a good life without any financial worries now, and without *him* into the bargain. He didn't give a damn about his father bequeathing her the money. It was what it might lead to that he was having grim thoughts about.

No doubt in the weeks to come he would find out if his forebodings were well founded and until such time he would keep his own counsel and live one day at a time.

She'd read his mind back there beside the helipad but hadn't understood the reasons for his behaviour. He didn't want to control her. Had learnt a bitter lesson from giving in to pride.

When he'd come back to London he'd had no idea whether Kerry would want to discuss mending the break in their marriage, but once he'd seen Rosalie he'd known that, for good or bad, he was there to stay.

He was the limit, Kerry thought as she followed him. If Piers wasn't bothered about the money, what *was* he bothered about? Something was getting to him.

She felt like weeping every time she thought about Daniel's generosity. He'd remembered her in his will because at that time he hadn't known if she and Piers would ever be reconciled, and it was beginning to look as if his forward thinking was going to bear fruit, as after today she couldn't see herself ever understanding the man she'd married.

As the summer progressed towards shorter days and longer nights, Kerry had made no mention of looking for a place of her own in the light of her improved circumstances, but Piers wasn't convinced that she wasn't going to.

Since that frustrating discussion after the solicitor's phone call they were going through the motions with regard to their jobs and when they were with Rosalie, but apart from that there was little contact between them.

Meals were strained affairs and Kerry was tempted a few times to remind him that he had been the one to point out that children were very susceptible to atmosphere, but did she want any more confrontations? No!

Once Rosalie was settled for the night Piers left the house, usually returning when Kerry had gone to bed. It was a pattern that had developed after that first night when he'd disappeared while she'd been in the

bath and looked like continuing. Where he went she
didn't know and was determined not to ask. The message was coming over once again that she was there
on sufferance. That when their daughter was awake
he was happy to be there, but the moment she was
asleep he had other places he preferred to be.

Yet he never smelt of perfume or had lipstick on
his collar in the time-honoured tradition of the phi-
landering husband. But who was showing a lack of
trust now? she asked herself. Piers might be just walking the streets in his haste to get away from her, or
sitting all alone in a bar somewhere.

Wherever he went she wished she knew what was
eating at him. He'd made no secret of the fact that he
wasn't happy about Daniel leaving her the money,
even though he'd insisted he didn't object in principle. So what *was* the problem.

What are these?' Piers asked tightly one night when
they went into the sitting room, having cleared away
after the evening meal.

He'd picked up a handful of estate agent's brochures that he'd found on the sofa and was observing
her challengingly.

Kerry stared at him. 'I've no idea. What *are* they?'

'You've left them there because you didn't want to
have to tell me yourself, I suppose. Taking the easy
way out.'

'I haven't the slightest idea what you're talking
about.'

He waved them under her nose.

'They're brochures for houses that are for sale.'

'So what? They will belong to Lizzie. She's been looking for a bigger place.'

'So they're not yours?'

'No! Why should they be?'

'I just thought that...' His voice trailed away and suddenly she understood.

'Of course! That's it, isn't it? You thought that now I can afford it I'm going to get a place of my own, go back on my word. Well, you were wrong. But after being accused of something I had no intention of doing, I might just have a rethink now that you've put the idea into my head.'

'Whatever you decide to do, Rosalie stays here,' he said flatly. 'As I've told you before, I've missed out on two years of her life and I'm not going to be denied any more time with her.'

Was this what had been bugging him? she thought in bleak amazement. The fear that she would leave and take Rosalie with her? Was he blind? Couldn't he see that where *he* was, *she* wanted to be. But as she'd thought before, Piers only wanted his daughter.

'I wonder what your father would think if he heard us,' Kerry said as tears threatened. 'At each other's throats all the time over imaginary grievances. You still don't trust me, do you, if you think I would be plotting to buy a place of my own without telling you?'

'I'm sorry,' he said contritely, and took a step towards her, but she reached out as if to push him back and his eyes were bleak. 'Suit yourself,' he said coolly, and moved towards the front door.

'Just a moment!' she cried. 'You've walked out of here in the evening too often, leaving me to my own miserable thoughts. Well, now it's *my* turn. *You* can stay in tonight and see what it feels like to be left high and dry!' And she flung herself past him and up the stairs.

When she came down Piers was reading one of the evening papers and didn't look up until she said, 'In your own words, don't wait up for me.'

He lifted his head slowly and she watched his eyes darken. 'You shouldn't be out alone looking like that,' he said as he took note of the snug-fitting, pale blue linen suit she'd changed into, and the sheer stockings and high-heeled strappy sandals.

'Why not?'

'You know why not. You're too damned fanciable.'

'By everyone but you, it would seem,' she snapped, and that brought him to his feet. He was across the room before she could stop him and his arms were around her, his mouth on hers.

His first kiss was bitter-sweet. A reminder of past joys and desires fulfilled. The second caused an explosion of feeling between them like nothing Kerry had ever known before. They were so hungry for each other there was no time to go upstairs. They made love on the sitting-room floor with all the aching familiarity of before and yet with a pulsating newness that came from the long abstinence they had brought upon themselves.

There was tenderness and urgency in her and relief that, if nothing else, the physical magic hadn't gone. He was the only one she would ever want to share this kind of moment with, Kerry thought. His lean strength upon her was just as desirable as it had ever been. His kisses the only ones she wanted. Yet they had condemned themselves to live in a loveless desert, where moments like this were as far apart as oases.

She had always worn the same perfume and as Piers kissed the soft cleft between her breasts the smell of it was there, tantalising and familiar, reminding him of all those other times when he'd held her naked in his arms, before he'd gone storming off, afraid to admit that his marriage wasn't working.

When it was over they lay side by side without speaking and in the silence Kerry thought that never in all the times they'd made love had there been such a torrent of feeling. So what now? Where did they go from there? Was it time for a fresh start? Or was all they had left the satisfying of desire, the easing of the body?

As if he'd guessed her thoughts, Piers got slowly to his feet and looking down at her, said, 'If that seemed like me taking control again, I'm sorry. I got carried away.'

As their glances held Kerry knew that a fresh start was not going to be the automatic follow-on to what had just happened. It would seem that Piers was already regretting it, and wasn't prepared to discuss it, as he was doing what he'd done before when he hadn't wanted to talk, going into the study and closing the door.

Then she was flinging her clothes back on, straightening her hair and rushing out into the summer dusk, thinking wretchedly as she flagged down a taxi that before and since their separation Piers had developed a rare talent for demoralising her.

He'd said earlier that she could live where she wanted as long as he had Rosalie. That had been the first hurt, and now he was treating those enchanted moments they'd just shared as if they'd been a mistake.

Where *did* they go from here? Maybe she *should* move out, but she couldn't face a wrangle over their child. Rosalie deserved better than that and Piers had his rights just as she did.

Whatever is wrong?' Lizzie asked when she opened the door to find Kerry on the step. 'You look ghastly.'

'I feel it,' Kerry said, and looked around the apartment. 'Are you alone?'

'Yes. So take a seat, Kerry, and I'll get you a drink. Then you can tell me what's wrong.'

'We've just made love, Piers and I,' she said flatly when they were settled.

'So?' Lizzie exclaimed. 'What's wrong with that.'

'Nothing. Or so it seemed at the time. But the moment it was over he started apologising, as if it had been a mistake. And then went and shut himself in the study instead of giving us the chance to talk. And now I feel used and even more miserable than before. It was a moment I'd longed for, but like everything else in our lives it was flawed.'

'Was that how you felt at the time?'

'No. It was like nothing I've ever known before. Even better than it used to be. Like a trip to the stars. And I was sure he must have felt the same, but it didn't seem like it. I need to get out of there, Lizzie, but if I do he'll fight me tooth and nail for Rosalie and I can't bear that she should be dragged into our squabbles.'

'If you still love Piers and it is clear that you do, stay where you are,' Lizzie advised. 'Don't widen the breach. You two are meant to be together. I've seen the way he looks at you and it's the way a man looks at the woman he loves. All right, he might be difficult to understand at times but Piers Jefferson is, or was, proud and decisive, a one-woman kind of man, and *you* are that woman. So hang on in there.'

'I wish I could believe that.'

'You have to. Does he know where you are?'

Kerry shook her head.

'No. I had to get out of the house for a while and I came straight here by taxi.'

'So should we let him know where you are?'

She managed a grimace of a smile. 'No. I don't see why. I was intending to go out in any case, though I hadn't decided where to. It was a matter of making a gesture. Piers has been disappearing every night after we've eaten and I don't know where he goes. So to-night I told him that it was my turn and it was when I came downstairs ready to go out that the temperature rose.'

'I'm not surprised, having seen the outfit.' Lizzie said. 'You look fantastic.'

Kerry sighed. 'It's incredible that *either* of us can work up the enthusiasm for socialising after the twelve-hour shifts that we work, yet I thought if he can do it, so can I. But it all went out of control.'

'Go back home,' Lizzie coaxed. 'They *both* need you, Piers and Rosalie. That's where your place is, with them.'

'I wish I had your confidence regarding that,' Kerry told her, 'but I'll do as you say. For one thing, I have nowhere else to go at this time of night.'

When Kerry got back the only light showing from the outside of the house was from the lamp they kept switched on in Rosalie's room, so it appeared that Piers had gone to bed. She breathed a sigh of relief. Another confrontation was the last thing she wanted.

But she was presuming too much. When she went into the nursery to check on its tiny occupant he came up behind her on bare feet, dressed in just the boxer shorts he slept in.

Under other circumstances she might have been aroused, but not after his earlier comments after they'd made love. The pleasure of their earlier passion had been short-lived and a repeat of that was not what she wanted.

'So you're back,' he said flatly.

'Yes. I'm back, and you'll be surprised to know that no one "fancied" me.'

'That would depend on where you went, I suppose.'

'I went to Lizzie's if you must know. *My* movements are no secret.'

'And mine are?'

'I don't remember you ever saying where you disappear to every night when you can't get away quickly enough once we've eaten.'

They were whispering so as not to wake Rosalie and he beckoned her out onto the landing.

'And I don't remember you ever asking.'

'I shouldn't have to. We're living in the same

house. Sharing our responsibilities to our child. If I needed you I wouldn't know where to find you. I wouldn't know which club or bar to look in.'

'So you've assumed that when I leave here I'm out on the town. I suppose it was to be expected as I thought that *you* might have been doing the same kind of thing tonight. The night life of the city doesn't appeal to me any more. You would have been searching in the wrong places.'

So had he been tucked up with someone else? she thought miserably. Perhaps he thought that what had been sauce for the goose could be sauce for the gander.

'All right. I was wrong,' she said wearily. 'Don't bother to explain any further as I don't want to know.'

He shrugged.

'Fair enough. I'll say goodnight, then.' And he padded back into his room and left her to her thoughts.

She was still awake when the phone down in the hall rang half an hour later, and as there were no signs of life coming from Piers's room she went down to answer it.

'Is Piers available at all?' a youthful woman's voice said in her ear when she picked up the receiver.

'Who is that?' Kerry asked warily.

'It's Natalie.'

'And you are?'

'I'm a friend. I was wondering if everything was all right as he didn't turn up tonight.'

'And where would that be?'

There was a pause and then the caller said uncomfortably, 'Er, Olivet House.'

She's expecting me to know where that is, Kerry

thought bleakly. Maybe Piers has told her that ours is a relationship of convenience, so she sees nothing wrong in phoning.

'He had another engagement,' she told her stonily, 'but I'm sure he'll be with you tomorrow.'

'Good. I'll look forward to that. Bye for now,' the woman at the other end of the line said breezily, and rang off.

Yes, I'm sure you will, Kerry thought grimly, deciding that she would very much like to have a look at the owner of the voice, who occupied her husband's evenings and early mornings…and what a nerve to ring him at home!

When she tried to trace the phone number of the mystery woman the recorded message said that the caller's number had been withheld and she thought wryly that, under the circumstances, it wasn't surprising.

She'd had enough peaks and valleys for one day, she thought as she returned to bed. Mental and physical exhaustion were making her feel light-headed. Their relationship might be frustrating, complex, often hurtful, but life with Piers was never dull.

After Kerry had gone rushing round to Lizzie's, Piers had spent the rest of the evening wishing he could take back what he'd said after they'd made love. The words had been sincere enough, with no intended hurt in them, but they'd only made things worse between them after their need of each other had been satisfied.

Kerry's taunt that he was the only one who wasn't attracted to her had made his iron control crumble and he'd done what he'd been longing to do for what seemed like an eternity of misery.

There wasn't a moment in the day when he didn't ache to hold her, and at night it was torment to know she was so near yet so far. But the knowledge that he'd sacrificed his marriage for his pride was still there. It was something he had to live with. He admitted to himself that he'd used Cosgrove as the excuse for leaving her, when all the time it had been his pride and arrogance that hadn't let him admit that his marriage had been failing.

But Kerry had seen what he'd said as a cheapening of those moments when they'd given in to their longing and had left the house afterwards as if she couldn't get away quickly enough. Why was it that he never said what was in his heart? Was the old arrogance still there?

The next morning Kerry decided before the day had barely got under way that if Piers showed any signs of disappearing that evening she was going to follow him, and take Rosalie with her.

She would make sure that the little one had a good sleep in the afternoon and would keep her up later than usual when it was her bedtime. It was one of her days off duty so the opportunity was there for her to act if the moment arose.

On the face of it, what she was planning to do was degrading, but she had to find out what was happening. She'd told Piers she didn't want to know but it was far from the truth.

He'd been his usual self at breakfast and had made no reference to the previous night's happenings. He was a cool customer, this husband of hers, she'd thought, but Piers had always been a law unto himself.

It was obvious he hadn't heard the phone ring the night before or he would have asked who had called, and there was no way she was going to tell him.

So when breakfast was over she and Rosalie waved him off and then went back inside to start *their* day.

CHAPTER FIVE

WHEN Piers picked up his car keys that evening Kerry felt her heartbeat quicken. Rosalie was still up, having had her afternoon nap, and usually he didn't leave the house until she was asleep. But tonight it seemed that he felt the need to be off and she thought that having been denied the company of the mysterious Natalie the night before, he was out to make up for lost time.

'I'm off,' he said. 'See you tomorrow.'

She made no reply, just nodded and thought that he might be seeing her sooner than he expected if she didn't lose track of him when he set off for wherever he was going. He was a fast and confident driver and it wouldn't be easy to keep at a distance to avoid him realising she was following him and yet not lose sight of his car.

She had no way of knowing how far he would be going and had filled the petrol tank during the day, but she needn't have bothered. After only a mile or so he pulled up outside a large, drab-looking house and parked his car outside.

Her eyes widened. Huddled low in her seat, she watched him go in and thought that it didn't look much like a love nest. Her sense of purpose was weakening, but she wasn't going to turn back. She had to know what or who it was that took Piers away from her each evening for so many hours.

The door was unlocked and as she pushed it open

Kerry saw that the inside of the house was as drab as its exterior. As she hesitated in a musty-smelling hallway with Rosalie in her arms, she heard Piers laugh and the sound propelled her through double doors into a scene that she would never have expected to find in a thousand years.

In the short space of time since his arrival he'd donned a white coat and with a smiling brown-haired woman beside him that she presumed must be Natalie was sounding the chest of a grizzled old man.

He looked up as the doors clicked to behind her and after the first moment of surprise she saw a smile tug at his mouth.

'Kerry,' he said. 'And Rosalie. So you've caught up with me.'

He turned back to the bare-chested man and told him, 'You're not as chesty as last week when you seemed to be heading for bronchitis, Billy, but I want to see you again in a few days' time. Keep taking the antibiotics.'

'Aye, Doc,' he said, and ambled off through a door at the back that seemed to lead to a dining room of sorts.

'What is this place?' she breathed.

'Natalie will explain,' he said coolly. '*I've* got some more people to see. Natalie, why don't you take my wife into the rest room and tell her what it's all about?' he suggested to the woman beside him, and she nodded.

'Olivet House is a night refuge,' Natalie explained, 'for the homeless. I realised when I spoke to you last night that Piers hadn't told you what he's been doing.'

'No, he hadn't,' Kerry said, still in a state of disbelief. 'I don't understand how he comes to be here. He works long shifts in Accident and Emergency at one of the big hospitals in the city centre. So do I, for that matter. Don't you have your own medical staff?'

'We do have a GP that we can call on, but he isn't always available. Piers has been helping us on a voluntary basis and we've felt privileged to have his services.'

Kerry could feel tears pricking. Why did he always make her feel as if she was in the wrong? she wondered dismally. And why had she been so quick to think the worst of him? Piers hadn't been a bar-fly before so why should she have thought he'd turned into one now? Yet why couldn't he have told her where he'd been all those nights, instead of leaving her to fret all alone?

'We're going,' she told him a few minutes later. 'Rosalie is tired and I need to think.'

'There's nothing to think about,' he said, still in the same cool tone. 'The people who pass through this place need all the help they can get. That's why I offered my services. They're often suffering from malnutrition and chest complaints amongst other health problems, and although the local authorities are responsible for the upkeep, the funding they get just isn't enough. Natalie is a social worker who works nights here, and you can imagine what *she* has to deal with.

Kerry nodded. As usual Piers was articulate and persuasive. And she couldn't fault him. She just wished that once in a while he wanted to spend his evenings with her.

*   *   *

She was still up when he came in and he said, 'I thought you'd have gone to bed long ago.'

'I told you that I wanted to talk and though you were convinced there was nothing to say, I don't agree.'

He sighed. 'I know what you want to know. You're going to ask me why I didn't tell you where I was going each night.'

'Correct. Why didn't you? I would have thought I was entitled to know that, if nothing else. Natalie rang up last night after you'd gone to bed. She wanted to know why you hadn't turned up, and I thought you were having an affair.'

'I see,' he said slowly. 'So from thinking I was spending my time carousing around the pubs and clubs you changed to having me engaged in an adulterous relationship. I don't know which is the most insulting, though I think the other-woman scenario has it.

'I don't know why I didn't tell you where I was going each night, Kerry. You never asked, so I thought you weren't interested. That you were glad to see me go. Until last night when you challenged me about it. But when you didn't pursue it this morning I thought that nothing had changed and so I went round to the refuge as usual.'

'I never asked because I thought you would tell me that what you did in your spare time was your business,' she told him. 'And how could I complain when each night you'd helped me with the meal and then put Rosalie to bed before leaving the house? I just wish you'd told me, that's all.'

'I'm sorry,' he said levelly. 'Sorry about a lot of

things. I'll spend more of my time with Rosalie and you if you want me to. Apart from wanting to help, I started working at the refuge because I thought you needed some space away from me. That first day on the unit I heard someone discussing the place and thought if I could do some good there I would, while at the same time leaving your evenings free of me.'

Her face had softened and her voice was gentle as she told him, 'You are right about that, me wanting to see less of the controlling side of you, even though I realise that being how you are is what makes you excel in everything you do. It was what attracted me to you in the first place, but in the end it became the reason for the split.'

He sighed. 'I know. And I didn't excel when it came to marriage, did I? The reason I went storming off like I did was because I couldn't face a failed marriage.'

'I wasn't exactly a howling success either,' she admitted wryly. 'We were both all right as long as everything was going smoothly, but didn't function too well when it wasn't. It was as if all the things I'd loved about you in the beginning were combining to set me against you. And as for Danny Cosgrove, I was so determined to make a point that I missed what was under my nose, the fact that our marriage was floundering. You were right about him, you know. Danny was way below standard. I've been told that he's left the NHS and gone into market gardening.'

'That sounds more like him, watching plants grow,' he said with a grim smile.

'Possibly,' she agreed. 'But getting back to you giving me some space, as you describe it, in the evenings, I do value my independence. Bringing up a child alone has taught me how to stand on my own two feet. I know that your father was there for me, yet I was always aware that he wouldn't be around for ever, as recent events have proved.

'But, yes, Piers, I *would* like to spend some time with you in the evenings, and I would also be more than willing to share you with the refuge. How do you feel about that?'

His face had lightened and there was a lift to his voice as he said, 'I think it's a step in the right direction. We're talking sense for once.'

'Good,' she replied, 'and as it's long gone midnight and we both have a busy day tomorrow, I'll say goodnight.'

When Kerry had gone upstairs Piers went to make a coffee, and as he was filling the kettle he thought that she might not want him in her bed yet, but at least his wife wanted him near in the evenings.

As the days went by he was proved right. It *was* a step in the right direction.

Some nights they watched television together after Rosalie had gone to sleep, chose good books and lost themselves in their pages or chatted about the days happenings within a sort of calm cocoon that kept at bay such things as decision-making.

On other evenings Piers went to the refuge, and as she waved him off with an easy mind Kerry knew there would never be anyone else for her. Piers might have his prickly side, but no other man could equal him. Who else would take off into the chilly night to spend five or six hours treating the homeless after a long day in the operating theatre?

But always when it was time for bed they went to their separate rooms, as if they'd set that part of their lives on hold.

The familiar tell-tale signs were there. Queasiness in the morning, tender breasts and, most conclusive of all, no period. Kerry was pregnant and knew she shouldn't be surprised. They hadn't been prepared the night they'd made love. Nothing had mattered except their need for each other, and now she was carrying their child.

Piers wouldn't be able to accuse her of keeping this one secret, she thought as the days went by and a pregnancy test confirmed that she wasn't mistaken. But she wanted to keep it to herself for a little while as she had no idea how he would react when she told him.

He'd seemed regretful after they'd made love. Would he also have regrets about the results of that same love-making? As wonderful as it was, the timing wasn't right, an unplanned baby in their present circumstances. Piers loved Rosalie dearly, but would he see another child as a strengthening of the chains that bound him to them?

In the meantime, she concealed the nausea and tried not to let him see that anything was different. It wasn't easy. Every time she looked at Rosalie she wanted to tell her that she was going to have a little brother or sister. But in spite of some new degree of understanding, they weren't in the 'happy families' league…yet. She sometimes thought that maybe they

never would be. That the events of the past had put
too much of a blight on the future.

When she told Lizzie her first words were, 'Does
Piers know?'

'Not yet,' Kerry told her. 'I want some breathing
space before I tell him as I have no idea what he'll
say.'

'Having seen him with Rosalie, I would expect him
to be delighted,' Lizzie said, but Kerry shook her
head.

'He might be if this time it was planned, but it
wasn't, and he can be unpredictable.'

'Even so, don't leave him to find out for himself,'
her friend persisted. 'Once you start to show, you'll
have no choice but to tell him.'

She was two and half months pregnant and Kerry still
hadn't told Piers she was carrying their second child.
It was becoming harder with every day to find the
right words and the right moment but, as Lizzie kept
pointing out, soon the change in her shape would
speak for itself, and how would he react to that?

'You have to tell him,' she urged. 'For one thing,
it is his child as much as yours and he is entitled to
know, especially after what happened regarding
Rosalie's birth.'

'I know,' Kerry agreed despondently. 'I keep shirk-
ing it because I dread what it might do to our already
frail relationship. When we made love that night he
as good as said it had been a mistake. So is he going
to be dancing with joy when he discovers I'm pregnant?'

'He might be if you tell him before he finds out

for himself,' Lizzie said worriedly. 'And was that how *you* saw it?'

'No. It was incredible, as if we were one.'

'So maybe he felt the same and isn't saying.'

Kerry sighed. 'I wouldn't know. Piers never lets me see what's in his mind. He wasn't like that before. It was just the opposite, He was always at great pains to let me know what he thought about everything. But with regard to the baby I promise that I'll tell him some time today.'

This conversation took place at half past seven in the morning. Piers was upstairs getting dressed and Lizzie, who had just arrived to take care of Rosalie, had discovered that Kerry was too nauseous to eat any breakfast. It was that fact that had triggered off the discussion and now, having committed herself, Kerry knew there was no turning back. Lizzie was right. Piers deserved to know.

Kerry was pale, Piers thought as they went out to their cars. He hadn't seen her eat any breakfast and she'd seemed listless and preoccupied of late, except for when they were on the job, and then as the adrenalin surfaced she perked up.

He supposed he was to blame. Blundering back into her life when she'd got it all planned. What would his father think if he could see them? That they were dragging their feet after he'd created the opportunity for them to make a fresh start?

If there *was* something bothering her, he would wait until tonight and then ask what was wrong, he decided as he drove the short distance to the hospital with her car close behind his.

He wasn't to know it but nature was about to move matters along. The day had barely got under way when the helicopter arrived with an elderly man on board. He'd been knocked down by a car in the rush-hour and a CT scan showed there was a ruptured blood vessel in his head, causing a haematoma, which would mean drilling holes in the skull to drain the blood clot and then clipping the ruptured blood vessel.

He also had a fracture of the femur on his left-hand side, but first the surgeons needed to treat the head injury. The fracture wasn't life-threatening. The haematoma was.

Piers was aware of Kerry across from him as he operated, and he noticed that her pallor was even more pronounced, but it was not the moment to comment, with a life at stake.

At last it was over and the patient had been wheeled into Intensive Care. He wasn't young and might have died if he'd had to wait for treatment elsewhere, but prompt attention to his injuries had given the old man a chance and hopefully soon his relatives would appear, as a young nurse had been trying to contact them ever since he'd been brought in.

'It's not a good thing to be involved in an accident any time,' Piers said when the tricky surgery was over. 'But at this man's age it could leave him an invalid with little mobility. It's sad how one's life can be ruined in a matter of seconds.'

Was that a message for her? Kerry wondered. Telling her that was what had happened to him when he'd found her in Danny's arms. If it was, it wasn't the time to remind her. Her legs felt like jelly and the nausea was really getting to her.

Piers had peeled off his gloves and was washing his hands when he heard a sort of soft, sighing moan from behind him, and when he swivelled round he was just in time to catch Kerry before she crumpled on to the floor in a faint.

If she'd been pale before, she looked ghastly now, he thought anxiously, and wanted to kick himself for not doing something about it. But thankfully she was already opening her eyes and staring up at him blankly.

'Don't move,' he said gently.

'What happened?' she asked weakly.

'You fainted. There's something wrong, isn't there?'

She didn't answer and another nurse who'd hurried across when she'd seen her fall said with a smile, 'I don't think it's anything that nine months gestation won't cure, Piers. I heard her retching just after she got here and it's happened a few times. Kerry has all the appearance of being pregnant.'

As she listened to what the other nurse was saying from her horizontal position on the floor, Kerry closed her eyes again to shut out the disbelief on the face bending over her. If there had been one way she hadn't wanted Piers to discover she was pregnant, it was like this.

She'd been feeling faint and queasy ever since she'd got up, but it had eased off while she'd been working and just when she'd been about to go for something to eat it had come back, with the result that she'd fainted.

Unaware of the situation she'd just created, the other woman said enviously, 'Aren't you the lucky ones? My guy and I have been trying for ages but with no luck so far.' And on that note she left them to gather up the pieces of the shattered moment.

So far Piers hadn't spoken, but with the nurse's departure he was about to make up for it.

'How dumb could I be?' he exclaimed as Kerry eased herself upwards and leaned against the leg of a nearby table. 'I'm a doctor, for heaven's sake, and I couldn't see what was in front of my nose.' His voice hardened. 'Why didn't you tell me? Talk about history repeating itself! I suppose that everyone for miles around knows except me...the father. That is, presuming I *am* the father.'

Kerry looked around her, grateful that the rest of the team had taken advantage of a short lull in their working day and gone to eat. The bitterness was back, she thought dismally, and who could blame him? She should have taken notice of Lizzie and told him weeks ago, but there was a limit to what she was going to allow him to say.

'The only other person who knows I'm pregnant is Lizzie. And I think you are insulting,' she said weakly. 'Of course the baby is yours. How dare you suggest otherwise? Or have you forgotten that we made love one night without taking any precautions?'

'No. I haven't forgotten,' he said stonily.

'And that you seemed to think it was a mistake.'

'I don't remember saying that.'

'You said something to that effect if not those exact words, and that is why I've been reluctant to tell you. *Do* you want another child, Piers?'

'Of course I do!' he exclaimed. 'I can't think of anything I would like more.'

Relief was washing over her but she had to ask, 'With me as the mother?'

She was getting to her feet and he reached out to assist her, but she waved his arm away as she waited for his answer.

'How else? You're my wife. I'm not in the habit of mating with every woman I meet.'

She sensed it was there again. The suggestion that she was only there to be used…someone to give him children.

'So you've no regrets now that you know?' she questioned flatly. 'You don't want me to have a termination?'

She had no intention of doing any such thing, but in view of his attitude couldn't resist asking.

'I'll treat that question with the contempt it deserves,' he replied. 'And now how about you having something to eat? You *will* feel faint if you haven't eaten for hours. Afterwards I suggest you go home and rest and at the same time consider whether you should give up your job.'

'That is something I don't need to consider,' she said snappily. 'I am not giving up my job. If I find that it's too much when the baby is born then maybe, but not before.'

He shrugged. 'All right. Suit yourself. Just make sure the baby doesn't suffer in the process.'

'You are a cold fish, Piers!' she exclaimed. 'I think I preferred you when you were all fire and brimstone.'

She watched his face bleach and thought she saw

pain in the dark eyes looking into hers, but there was no sign of it in what he had to say next.

'The others will be back shortly. They're already curious about us and will be even more so if they find out that I didn't know you were pregnant. They have no idea of the kind of life we lead away from this place.'

'So?'

'So I suggest that you do what I said. Take the rest of the day off. You're a risk to yourself and others if you try to do this job when you're not on top form— and that's an order.'

'And you're good at giving those, aren't you?'

'Only when the need arises. So are you going, or do I have to see you off the premises personally?'

'I'm going, but it is just for this once. We both know that pregnancy is only dangerous when there are complications present, and apart from the nausea I am perfectly fit...*and* have no intention of putting the baby at risk. I'll see you tonight, Piers.' And with feelings that were a mixture of relief and annoyance, she went.

Lizzie and Rosalie had just come back from the park when she got in and her friend observed her in surprise.

'I fainted,' Kerry told her before she could ask, 'and one of the nurses who'd already twigged that I was pregnant let the cat out of the bag.'

'You mean that Piers knows?'

'Yes, he does.'

'And how did he react?'

'Typical Piers. He wasn't pleased to be told by

someone else that he was going to be a father again, but happy about the baby. That's a toned-down description of what happened, but basically correct.'

'And how was his attitude towards you?'

'The same as always. He even had the nerve to question if the child was his. He's *ordered* me to rest,' she said wryly, 'but I think it is more for the baby's sake than mine.'

'Have you thought that he might see this as a way of keeping you together?'

'What? In our farce of a marriage?'

'That might seem how it is,' Lizzie agreed, 'but which would you rather have—nothing or this?' Kerry knew there was only one answer to that. Even Piers at his most cool and remote was better than not being near him at all.

As the day wore on Piers was trying to get his mind around the fact that he and Kerry had made another child. It was a humbling thought that out of those moments of intense passion had come such a gift and he wished that the two of them were in harmony about it.

He was still smarting from the hurt of finding out the way he had, but understood why she'd not wanted to tell him, and he wondered just how long it would have been before the decision was taken out of her hands.

He'd said all the wrong things again, of course, and left Kerry feeling that she was merely a means to an end. She would almost certainly not believe him if he told her that he still loved her.

The thought of another baby on the way brought

with it the hope that she wouldn't move out. He couldn't demand it but the chances were greater and for that he was thankful.

The head of the trust came to see him in the late afternoon and announced that the hospital intended honouring his father by naming a new ward after him and placing a plaque just inside the entrance of the trauma unit.

'We'll want you and your family to be there, needless to say,' he said. 'To name the ward and unveil the plaque. It was such a terrible waste, losing Daniel like that, but at least it brought you to us, Piers.' As the top man had gone on his way Piers thought that it was good to know that someone was glad to have him around.

When he arrived home that evening Kerry was in the middle of preparing the meal and Rosalie, dressed in her pyjamas, was playing with her toys on the kitchen floor. But the moment she saw him she was on her feet with arms outstretched, toddling towards him.

This was what it was all about, he thought achingly, and he'd almost missed out on it because of his pride and stupidity. But the past *was* past. They were together again and he could wait for ever as long as he didn't lose Kerry again.

But instead of putting his thoughts into words, he merely said, 'Did you rest as I told you to?'

'Yes,' she replied. 'I had something to eat and then went to bed for a couple of hours. Lizzie has only just gone.'

'And how do you feel now?'

'Much better. Especially now that you know about the baby.'

He frowned. 'What sort of a monster do you think I am, Kerry? *You're* the one with the difficult part to play, while I just wait on the sidelines and get the prize in the end.'

She raised her head from chopping green beans and as their glances held said, 'You weren't talking like that earlier.'

'Maybe not. At the time I was trying to adjust to a very private matter concerning ourselves that had just been told to me by a casual acquaintance. But changing from a delicate subject to one not so delicate, though equally surprising, I was told this afternoon that the hospital is going to honour Dad by naming a ward after him and placing a plaque in the entrance to the trauma unit.'

There'd been a break in his voice and she knew how much it meant to him that his father should have been so respected. He turned away to conceal his emotion, and unable to help herself, she moved across to him and put her arms around him.

For a brief moment they were as one, united in their grief, and she said softly, 'I loved him, too, you know. He was a lovely man. Daniel was very kind to me. A true friend when I needed one.'

'Yes, I know,' he said tightly, moving out of her embrace. 'You don't have to keep reminding me of my shortcomings. If I'd known we had a child, Dad wouldn't have had to stand in for me. I would have been there myself.'

'And would you have had any second thoughts about coming back just for me?' she asked, hurt at the way he'd moved out of her arms and been snappy when all she'd done had been tell him how she'd loved his father.

He didn't reply. What was the point in telling her that he'd had second thoughts a thousand times, but had pushed them away when he'd remembered how he'd found her in that clown Cosgrove's arms? It had been the last straw, the final blow to his pride.

A pan was boiling over, unheeded in the mind battles that were going on in the sunlit kitchen, and a toddler was at his feet wanting to be picked up.

'Shall I tuck Rosalie up for the night while you rescue the vegetables?' he suggested, and Kerry nodded mutely. Child care and food were safe subjects.

It was two weeks later on a cool autumn evening when the ceremony to honour Daniel Jefferson was held and the boardroom at the hospital was crowded with those who'd known and loved him and weren't on duty.

Cocktails were being served first and then those assembled were going to gather outside the new ward that was to be named after him. Piers was going to cut a ribbon and proclaim that the latest addition to the hospital's facilities was to be called the Daniel Jefferson Ward.

When they'd talked about the presentation again after that first emotional discussion he had said that he would like Rosalie to pull the cord that would unveil the plaque in memory of her grandfather, and that time it had been Kerry fighting back the tears.

'We'll have to make sure that she has a sleep in the afternoon, or our young miss will be too tired to take out,' she'd told him.

'Whatever you say,' he'd agreed. 'I just want all my family to be there.' His glance had been on her already thickening waistline and he'd gone on to say, 'Even though one member of it has yet to put in an appearance.'

Kerry had observed him with puzzled eyes. If he felt like that he must have a weird idea of what real family life was like, she thought, as one of its main ingredients was a mother and father who slept in the same bed.

But she'd supposed that the fact that he *was* thinking along those lines was a step in the right direction and if they had different ideas of what the term meant, so be it.

And now the moment had arrived. Piers, who had himself well under control, cut the ribbon across the doorway of the new ward and then they all made their way to the trauma unit that had been Daniel's patch, the place where he had co-ordinated the best skills he could find to treat those who came to them from the city's highways and byways.

In a pretty new dress and fresh from a long sleep that afternoon, Rosalie had no idea what it was all about, but when she saw the golden cord dangling invitingly she strained forward in her father's arms and gave it the necessary pull.

It had been arranged so that tiny hands could release it and at the first tug the cover slid to one side and the plaque was revealed. Intrigued with the result of her efforts, she would have liked to have done it again and Piers had to step back out of reach.

Standing beside them, Kerry was thinking that this

was incredible. In a matter of weeks her life had changed so much she could hardly believe it. Daniel had gone. Piers was back and she had fallen pregnant, and their daughter had just completed her first public engagement.

So why wasn't she on top of the world? Was it because the front they were putting up for everyone wasn't what it appeared to be? Or was Piers thinking along the right lines and they *did* have a chance of salvaging something out of the mess they'd made?

CHAPTER SIX

As THEY drove home she could tell that Piers was content with the results of the evening. The presentation, Rosalie's part in it and them being together as a family.

He was smiling as he carried their sleepy child upstairs to bed, and when he came down again he said, 'What do you think Dad would have thought about tonight's affair?'

'He would have loved it,' Kerry told him. 'Not for the fact that he was being honoured, but because so many of those he'd worked with were there, and as the icing on the cake, amongst them his prodigal son and his granddaughter to do the honours.'

She hadn't mentioned herself and neither did he when he said, 'Yes. I think you're right.' So she was still the encumbrance that went with Rosalie, she thought.

Since he'd discovered she was pregnant Piers had done more of the chores around the house and was watching over her to make sure she didn't overdo it on the unit. She wondered just how much of his concern was directed at herself and how much of it was for the unborn child. Would the scales be evenly balanced if it came to the test? she asked herself.

The nausea had gone, as it often did once the first three months of the pregnancy had passed, but she soon felt tired and tonight was no exception after the emotional presentation.

'I'm off to bed.' she told him.

She saw disappointment in his glance, but the only thing he had to say was, 'Hadn't you better eat first? Those nibbles we had at the presentation weren't enough to feed two.'

She sighed. 'I'll get a glass of milk and a biscuit if it will put your mind at rest.' And marching into the kitchen, she did as promised.

When she went back to join him he asked, 'What's wrong? It's been a wonderful evening. Don't spoil it, Kerry.'

'I'm not going to.'

'But?'

'I feel as if *I* don't matter.'

'Would I be here if that was the case?'

'You might be. I imagine you would put up with anything to be near Rosalie.'

'Yes, it's true. I would. But that's a separate thing, my love for my daughter. It has nothing to do with the way I feel about you.'

'Exactly,' she said, and began to climb the stairs.

As Piers gazed sombrely after her he knew that Kerry thought he only wanted her around to give him children and he wanted to go after her and tell her that it wasn't so.

Yet it was true that he saw the child she was carrying as their hope of reconciliation. That he didn't see it entirely as Rosalie's sister or brother, or *their* son or daughter, but as a bridge that would span the gap that had formed between them. But it seemed as if Kerry saw his behaviour as self-motivated. That he was using her to suit his own ends. And if that *was* the case, they weren't there yet...

His father had been the supreme optimist if he'd thought it would be easy for them to forgive and forget, and as he followed her upstairs the longing was strong to go into her room and tell her that *she* was the one who mattered first and foremost. But after what she'd said earlier he doubted she would believe him.

The atmosphere at breakfast next morning, which was often subdued after a night spent in their separate bedrooms, was more relaxed than usual, as even the few sharp words they'd exchanged before going to bed hadn't been enough to wipe out the feelings of pride and affection that had been there the night before for a very special man.

For once Kerry was feeling almost light-hearted and as they walked briskly through the hospital's main entrance Piers said, 'You look chirpy this morning, considering we had words before going to bed. Any particular reason?'

She gave him a quick sideways glance. 'I keep thinking about the presentation. How we were there for Daniel, the three of us. It was a wonderful evening.'

'That *was* because we were there for Dad,' he said dryly. 'We had a common interest for once.'

He'd made the comment mildly enough but it upset her. There'd been the inference that they had no real rapport of their own and it had taken her mind back to the time when they'd lived for each other. Been so in love that stubbornness and pride hadn't had a chance to surface. Until Piers's scorn for a hapless young registrar and her subsequent defence of him had turned the fabric of their marriage into a battle-ground.

When she thought back, Kerry couldn't believe they could have been so stupid. They should have discussed their different points of view rationally, instead of being continually at flashpoint. But it had been as if they'd both suddenly discovered that the other was flawed and it hadn't been acceptable.

Yet she still believed that the rift would have healed if only he hadn't accused her of being unfaithful to him. The hurt of the false accusation had been the death knell to any hopes of them being reconciled.

It had been Danny's *arms* that he'd found her in—not his *bed*. But to Piers, enraged and jealous, it had been as good as, and after their biggest argument ever he'd packed his bags and left.

In the midst of her devastation she had become aware of feelings of nausea and tender breasts, just the same as it had been this time, and in a state of disbelief had faced up to the fact that she was pregnant.

Her first reaction had been one of joyful relief. When Piers knew he would come back, she'd told herself. He would never shut himself away from his child. But it hadn't been so simple. He'd disappeared and as the months had gone by she'd bitterly accepted that she was going to be faced with the role of single parent.

When Rosalie had been born she'd persuaded Daniel, with bitterness still persisting, not to tell his son that he had a child if Piers ever did turn up, and because he was aware of her hurt and devastation he'd reluctantly agreed. Until the fates had taken a hand in things and brought the only man she had ever loved back into her life.

Piers was observing her expression and asking himself why he always had to force a reaction out of Kerry. Awkward blighter that he was, he'd wiped the smile off her face. Made himself sound doubtful regarding the reason for their enjoyment of the previous night's presentation, when all the time every moment they spent in harmony was as precious as fine gold.

As he turned to tell her he was sorry for being so downbeat, the helicopter came whirring overhead and in the street down below the sirens of the fast response car were warning them that their day was about to begin. They quickened their steps and the moment was gone.

When they presented themselves on the unit they discovered that a minibus taking workers to a factory had collided with a taxi in the early morning traffic and the casualties from both vehicles had just arrived.

The taxi driver, who'd had to be cut free from his vehicle by the fire services, and a young woman were the most badly injured, and within minutes the team were swinging into action.

The taxi driver was on the operating table and as Piers looked down at him his face was sombre. He'd been scanned and X-rayed for damage to the heart and spine and the results had shown injuries in both areas from the impact of the front of the minibus ramming his vehicle head on.

There was other damage, too, causing heavy blood

loss, and as the combination of surgeons, radiologists, anaesthetists and nurses prepared to swing into action it was another life at stake, another member of the public receiving the fastest care available.

The woman's injuries were serious but not as life-threatening as the taxi driver's, and as Piers evaluated what was going to be needed to save his life, other members of the team were treating her for a fractured pelvis and head injuries.

As always, he was aware of Kerry at the other side of the table, poised and watchful, tuned in to the urgency of the moment and he flashed her a brief smile.

He never forgot for a moment that she was carrying their child. Rosalie was the bond that bound them now, but this new baby was his hope for the future. A future in which they would be together for the right reasons. Not because they'd brought children into the world, but because they couldn't exist without each other.

The taxi driver was given transfusions to replace the serious blood loss and then prepared for cardiac surgery to repair a damaged heart valve, and after considering the extent of the injuries to the spinal vertebrae it had been decided that the orthopaedic surgeon on the team would try realignment of the bones in the hope that further extensive surgery might be avoided, or at the least delayed until his general condition was more stable. Methylprednisolone would then be given to him to ease inflammation and it would be wait-and-see time. His other injuries, serious enough but minor compared to the heart and spine problems, would then be assessed and dealt with.

His wife had been contacted and was anxiously

waiting outside the unit for news. 'How could this have happened?' she choked. 'My Dave is such a good driver.'

'That doesn't take into account the risk from those who aren't so good,' Kerry told her gently. 'We're doing all we can for your husband. Dave has got some of the best in the land working on him. If anyone can give him a fighting chance they can, so hang in there.'

Two weeks later the woman had been discharged and the taxi driver was making slow but satisfactory progress from the surgery and the various fractures he'd suffered in the accident. The alignment of the vertebrae was being sustained and one day soon he was hoping to be on his feet again and mobile.

A burly father of four, he was never short of visitors. His family were constantly by his bedside and fellow members of the taxi-driving fraternity popped in from time to time.

On a rare occasion when he was alone, Kerry stopped for a quick chat on her way to the staffroom and as always was amazed by his stoicism. The accident that had caused him to almost lose his life and was now leaving him without any immediate livelihood was enough to depress most people, especially as the minibus driver had been the one at fault.

But he had accepted what had happened with a sort of fatalistic calm, which she thought was explained when he said, 'As long as nothing happens to the wife and kids, I can cope. They are my life. Angie and I have never been apart for a night since we got married...until now. But one day soon we'll be back as we were and I'm truly grateful to you folks for what you did for me.'

She'd gone on her way thinking that it was more than she and Piers could say. They'd spent many nights apart. They were still doing so, and all for the most stupid of reasons, while this family had got it right. She wished that Piers could have been there to hear what the injured man had said.

But maybe the taxi driver and his wife didn't demand so much of each other as she and Piers did. Perhaps *they* knew the meaning of tolerance and forgiveness.

In the middle of the following night Kerry woke up with stomach cramps and immediately alarm bells started to ring, especially when she saw that there was blood spotting.

As she stood in the bathroom, taking in what was happening, it was as if the word 'miscarriage' was blotting out all coherent thought except that she needed to return to bed to get off her feet while she calmed down.

When she went back onto the landing, with her mind trying to take in what was happening, Piers came out of his room with a question in his eyes.

'You're awake,' she said weakly.

He nodded. 'Yes. I don't sleep well these days. I hear Rosalie if she only turns over, and I thought I heard you cry out. Is anything wrong?'

She wasn't going to be able to keep this from him she was thinking, but wished that she could. Piers would be devastated if they lost this child...and so would she, but as usual she put his needs first.

'I've got stomach cramps and I'm spotting,' she told him with dismal baldness, and watched his expression change from mild curiosity to alarm.

'Then why are you standing there?' he said immediately. 'Let's get you back into bed and send for a doctor.'

'Morning will do,' she said flatly, longing for him to hold her close and tell her it was going to be all right.

'No. It won't,' he contradicted tightly. 'We're not taking any chances. In fact, we'll go one better than getting an emergency doctor out. I'll take you to the hospital. That's where you need to be with those kind of symptoms.'

'But I'm not haemorrhaging heavily and I've had worse gripes than this when I'm menstruating,' she protested, knowing that she was letting his manner make her play down her own anxiety.

'This is our child we're talking about,' he said with the tightness still in him, 'so don't make light of what's happening, Kerry.'

Her face flamed. The note of censure that she hated was there in his voice.

'I'm not doing that. I just don't want to make a fuss about nothing. I'll pack a bag and we'll do as you say. But what about Rosalie?'

'We'll wrap her in a blanket and take her with us,' he said calmly, now that he'd got his own way, and Kerry thought that this was Piers in control. She needed comfort and kindness. Not orders rapped out at her.

He barely spoke on the way to the hospital, except for remarking when she turned to check on Rosalie, who was fast asleep on the back seat, that she was all right and asking her how the pains were.

'Still there, but no worse at the moment,' she said, with a brevity to match his.

Piers was sick with anxiety. He wanted this baby with all his heart. It was going to make the family he loved complete, but only as long as no harm came to Kerry. Yet what was he doing? Behaving like an unsympathetic moron. And as if to confirm it she said suddenly, 'I must be insane, wanting to bring another child into this thing we call a marriage.'

His hands tightened on the steering-wheel, but he didn't reply, just gazed straight ahead and when she followed his glance Kerry saw the illuminated sign for A and E looming up in front of them in the dark autumn night.

She was in bed in a cubicle in the emergency area with Rosalie, still asleep, beside her on a big leather chair and Piers looking strained and sombre standing a few paces away as they waited for a gynaecologist to appear.

When he did he said, 'You've done the best thing, coming straight to us, Kerry. It could be a threatened miscarriage, yet lots of women have minor bleeding during pregnancy and still go to full term to produce a healthy baby. I'm going to send you for an ultrasound to check if it is an ectopic pregnancy, and if that isn't the case, to make sure that the baby is developing naturally.

'Also I think we'll do a pelvic examination to check if the size of the uterus is going to be a problem. Better to find out sooner than later.' And he patted her hand reassuringly before turning to Piers and saying, 'I believe you're both with the trauma unit upstairs.'

'Er…yes, we are,' he told him impatiently. 'So what are you saying? Is my wife on the verge of a miscarriage?'

The other man shrugged and Kerry knew that wouldn't go down well with Piers.

'We'll have a better idea when we've done the tests,' he said. 'In the meantime, we're going to keep you here, Kerry. It's bed rest for you until then.'

'Take Rosalie home,' she begged Piers. 'I don't want Lizzie to turn up in the morning and find the place empty.'

He looked as if he might refuse for a moment and then, as if he'd thought better of it, said, 'All right, but you send for me immediately if anything further develops. Promise?'

'Yes, of course I will,' she said wearily. 'I know how much *the baby* means to you. But Rosalie should be at home in her own bed, not wrapped in a blanket on a strange chair. *My* thoughts aren't only for those yet to come.'

'And you think mine are?' he said grimly, as he picked up his sleeping daughter and held her close.

'I don't know what *you* think, Piers,' she told him bleakly. 'I wish I did.'

Kerry was on the gynaecological ward for three days. Lizzie was taking care of Rosalie as usual during the day and Piers took over in the evenings, which made it difficult for him to visit. But he made up for it in the daytime by appearing by her bed every moment he could spare, which would have made her totally happy if it hadn't been for those first hours when she'd thought a miscarriage might be about to happen and he'd been so abrupt.

The tests had shown that the pregnancy was progressing satisfactorily with no abnormalities.

'Take a couple of weeks off,' the gynaecologist said. 'I'm told that the bleeding has stopped so unless it occurs again you should be all right. You can go home to that doting husband of yours, but take care. Don't overdo it when you go back to work.'

As she repacked the small case that she'd taken in with her, Kerry thought that the consultant must have seen something that she hadn't if he thought that Piers was 'doting'. With his daughter, yes, but not his wife.

Yet he'd brought her flowers and a photograph of Rosalie to put beside her bed, and had even kissed her briefly on an occasion when one of the team from A and E had popped in to see her.

Once Piers knew that the baby was safe and that Kerry wasn't going to be submitted to the pain and distress of a miscarriage, he had calmed down, but the scare had unnerved him. Made him less confident about how the next six months or so were going to be.

Each time he went to see her she looked pale and miserable, and he wasn't sure if it was due to anxiety over the baby or because he wasn't coming up to scratch as the loving husband. He was not normally short on speech. Far from it. But he had been of late, when it came to Kerry and himself.

In the early days of their marriage they'd told each other everything. Talked about their feelings, their hopes, their dreams. But now he felt that every time he had something to say he put his foot in it. That he'd forfeited the right to ever be so close again.

When he got the message to say she could go home, he was operating and knew that he wouldn't be finished for some time.

'Tell my wife I'll come and get her as soon as I'm free,' he told the nurse who'd rung, 'but it will be after lunch, I'm afraid, as I'm in the middle of surgery.'

Piers was smiling as he went back to his task. His world was righting itself. The baby was safe and the pivot on which his life and Rosalie's were hinged would be back in her room across the landing that night.

His expression was tender. He would take Kerry home and cherish her as she deserved to be cherished. Tonight they would talk. Clear away the cobwebs. The time was right. He could feel it in his bones.

It was two o'clock in the afternoon when he arrived on the ward and was told that Kerry had left in the middle of the morning. Disappointment engulfed him. He accepted that it was reasonable enough for her not to want to be in the place any longer than need be, with Rosalie waiting for her at home, but thought that she could have at least phoned up to the unit to say she didn't want to wait, thereby saving him the hours of anticipation that had come to nothing. Maybe she'd asked Lizzie to come for her or got a taxi. He intended to find out and when he asked, a young nurse told him, 'Mrs Jefferson rang for a taxi.'

'Fine,' he said, and instead of taking the afternoon off, as he'd intended, he went back upstairs to the unit. Kerry would have Lizzie there and Rosalie, he thought flatly. It would be like it had been before he'd appeared on the scene. They'd been managing very well without him then and were probably doing so now.

It was five o'clock when he got home and he found the two women and Rosalie in the back garden, taking advantage of what was left of the autumn sun. Kerry was lying on a sun lounger with Rosalie nearby and Lizzie was taking the washing off the line which he'd laundered the night before and hung out first thing before leaving the house.

When she saw him coming down the path towards them, Kerry felt herself tensing. There was something about the set of his jaw that told her he wasn't at his most relaxed and she said immediately, 'I'm sorry I didn't wait for you, Piers. I was so desperate to be with Rosalie I couldn't wait until this afternoon. You did get my message, didn't you?'

'No. I didn't, as a matter of fact,' he said, swinging Rosalie up into his arms. 'Who did you speak to?'

'One of the nurses. She said you were operating and she would pass it on.'

He was ashamed for thinking that Kerry would have just gone without a word when he'd so wanted to share the precious moment of her homecoming, and he *did* understand her eagerness to be with Rosalie. Lizzie had taken her in to see her mother each day, but for Kerry it hadn't been the same as being here at home with her. Yet the feeling of disappointment and being left on the outside was still there.

Lizzie had finished folding the washing and she smiled across at him.

'This is more like it, isn't it, Piers?' she said. 'Kerry back home where she belongs.'

'It is indeed,' he said evenly, adding to his wife, 'I'll go and make a start on the meal. Would you like to join us, Lizzie?'

The last thing he wanted tonight was company, but without Lizzie's help they would have had big problems over the last few days and he was thinking that Kerry might be glad to have her friend there as it would delay any close contact with him for a while.

'No, thanks.' she said quickly. 'I'm sure that the two of you are looking forward to some time together after the last few anxious days.' She turned to Kerry. 'I'll be here bright and early in the morning. Don't get up. Remember what the gynaecologist said.'

Kerry smiled and Piers wished she was as easy with him as she was with Lizzie. But Lizzie had never done anything to hurt or humiliate her, had she?

'You're annoyed I didn't wait for you, aren't you?' Kerry said when she'd gone. 'I thought you'd understand that I didn't want to be away from Rosalie any longer than I had to.'

'I do. No need to fret,' he told her, and, picking up the pile of ironing from the patio table where Lizzie had left it, he went into the house.

Kerry felt tears prick. They'd just gone through a stressful few days. Both of them apprehensive about the baby. But not united in their anxieties as they should have been. If only Piers would tell her what he was thinking. She knew he was happy to have her back under the same roof with him. But that could be for a variety of reasons.

Kerry woke up in the night and found him standing beside her bed, and as she looked up at him in drowsy surprise he said, 'I thought I heard you call out.'

She shook her head and raised herself up on the pillows. As he observed her smooth shoulders and the face above them he thought that she'd never been more beautiful, this wife of his that he'd cast aside like an old shoe in what seemed like another lifetime.

'No. I'm fine,' she told him. With a sudden rush of tenderness she took his hand in hers. 'We can't live on a knife edge for the next six months because of the scare that we've just had, Piers.' She said with a show of confidence that was more for his peace of mind than her own. 'I intend to carry this baby to full term. If I've nothing else to offer you, I *can* give you children, and that's what you want, isn't it?'

He'd sensed the tenderness in her and been about to take her in his arms and tell her how much she meant to him, but the chiller had been there in what she'd just said. Kerry was making it clear that having his child was fine, but nothing else was on offer. No sincere loving endearments. No passion to equal that never-to-be-forgotten occasion when the baby had been conceived.

He withdrew his hand from hers and in the darkened bedroom gave her the answer she was expecting.

'Yes, that *is* what I want,' he told her. 'Go back to sleep. I'm sorry I disturbed you.'

'Don't be,' she said softly as she eased herself back down beneath the covers. 'But do remember what I said. We are going to have this child. Rosalie needs a brother or sister.' And before he could reply to that she turned her head into the pillow and slept.

On her first morning back on the unit after her stay on the gynaecological ward Kerry was waiting for the lift when she saw Miles and Ria, the couple whose wedding day had been ruined by the explosion at the apartment block. They were coming out of Outpatients and when they saw her they came over.

When Kerry asked about his arm, Miles said, 'It's healing, thank goodness, and I've got some of the use back in it. The doctor we've just seen said that I may never get it back fully, but that the microsurgery has been as successful as it can be and I'm thankful for that.'

Kerry nodded. 'That is good. You came very near to losing your arm.' She glanced at Ria. 'What have you done about the wedding?'

The girl smiled. 'It's on Saturday. Just a quiet affair at the registry office. You may remember me telling you that neither of us have any family, so there's no point in making a big fuss. A couple of friends are standing for us and then we're flying to one of the Greek islands immediately afterwards.

'I don't suppose you'd like to come, would you— Mr Jefferson and yourself?' she asked with a sort of hesitant wistfulness and Kerry thought, poor girl, to have no family with her on her big day.

'If you'd like us to be there, we'd be honoured,'

she told her. 'As long as you don't mind us bringing our little girl. What time is the wedding…and where?'

'It's at two o'clock and the registry office is just a couple of blocks away from here.'

'Right. So we'll see you both there, then,' she said, and hoped that Piers would be as keen as she was to attend the wedding of two comparative strangers.

She was smiling when she arrived on the unit and he said, 'I was nearly coming to look for you. Are you all right?'

'Mmm. Couldn't be better. We've just been invited to a wedding.'

Dark brows rose as he took in what she'd said.

'A wedding? Whose?'

'You remember Miles, who almost lost his arm in the explosion at the apartment block?'

'Yes.'

'And that he and Ria should have been getting married the next day?'

'Yes.'

'Well, the cancelled wedding is taking place on Saturday, and as they have no families they've asked us if we will be present. I've said yes. I hope that's all right with you.'

'And where was all this arranged?'

'Just now. In the corridor outside Outpatients.'

'And the arm?'

'Healing, and Miles has some movement in it.'

It was Piers's turn to smile now.

'That's good news, and, yes, I'd like to go to their wedding. It's rare that we hear anything further from those we've treated. It's the staff on the wards and in Outpatients who get all the feedback.'

*   *   *

Ria had chosen to wear the full regalia for her wedding to Miles in spite of the lack of guests, and when she appeared in a bridal gown of stiff white brocade, with a shoulder-length veil and carrying a bouquet of freesias, Kerry flashed her a reassuring smile.

It wasn't all that long since Ria had been sobbing in a waiting room at the hospital, she thought, while Piers and the other surgeons had fought to save Miles's arm, and now here she was, young, beautiful and happy. It reminded her of the vows that Piers and herself had made and not kept.

Seated beside him and Rosalie in a tastefully decorated room in the municipal building that was licenced to perform marriages, Kerry wondered if he was thinking the same thing.

Yet she *had* kept only to him. Maybe she hadn't *obeyed* him as much as he would have liked, but she had certainly loved and cherished him and would have continued to do so if he had let her.

As Piers listened to the age-old vows he was wondering what Kerry would say if he suggested that they make *their* promises again and deciding that she would probably think he was crazy.

A pale sun had come out by the time the ceremony was over and as Ria and Miles stood outside on the steps for photographs with their five guests beside them, crazy or not, Piers couldn't get the idea out of his head.

CHAPTER SEVEN

DAVE, the taxi driver, was due to be discharged on a chilly November morning, and as they'd chatted a few times while he'd been in the hospital Kerry went on to his ward to say goodbye.

He had recovered from his injuries to some extent, but was still not as mobile as he would like to be and was supporting himself on two sticks when she found him talking to the ward manager as he waited for his family to come for him.

'This is the day I've been looking forward to,' he said when she appeared. 'I thought it would never come.' He gave a happy smile. 'Tonight I'll be with Angie in our king-sized bed, back where I belong with my family.'

'They mean a lot to you, don't they?' she said, and watched his smile turn to tears.

'They do indeed,' he agreed. 'They are my life, and if it hadn't been for everyone here I might never have seen them again. Angie is bringing a big cake and some wine for the ward staff and you people in A and E. I hope you'll have time to have a drink on me.'

At that moment Piers came striding on to the ward, and when he saw the taxi driver wiping his eyes he said quizzically, 'So what's going on here? You're not upsetting out star patient, are you, Kerry?'

'Course not,' Dave told him. 'We were just talking

about families. I was saying how much mine mean to me. My wife is bringing some goodies in. Will you have time to spare for a piece of cake and a drink, Mr Jefferson?'

'I most certainly will,' Piers told him, 'and if I don't get the chance to speak to you again before you leave, maybe you'll pop in and see us some time when you've been to Outpatients.'

'You can bank on it,' the big fellow told him. 'When the time comes, me and the missus will be wanting to know whether you've been blessed with another girl or a boy.'

In the lift going back up to the unit Kerry was straight-faced and silent, and after glancing at her a couple of times Piers said, 'What's wrong?'

'Nothing,' she told him.

He sighed. 'Don't expect me to believe that, Kerry. Was it something I said down there?'

She shook her head. 'No. It was listening to Dave talking about his family. It made me feel that, compared to his, ours is a poor thing.'

'And whose fault is that?'

'Need you ask? *Yours and mine.*'

'So what do you suggest we do about it.'

'Improve our communication maybe.'

'So you think we need to talk?'

'Yes, and not about Rosalie, the refuge, this place…or what we're going to have for dinner tomorrow. Let's talk about *us*.'

'Fine by me,' he said levelly, and once again the idea of taking their vows for a second time came to mind. 'Tonight, then?'

'Yes, tonight,' she agreed.

✝   ✳   ✳

The moment had come. Rosalie was asleep and now Kerry was wishing she hadn't suggested it. Supposing Piers had something to say that she didn't want to hear?

They were seated opposite each other in the sitting room, and patting the sofa beside him, Piers said, 'Come and sit over here.'

Kerry got to her feet reluctantly and went to sit beside him, deciding as she did so that if they were going to be so close she wouldn't be able to think straight.

'Right,' he said, once she was settled by his side. 'So what has Dave the taxi driver got that we haven't?'

She had her answer ready. 'Contentment. A king-sized bed. A wife that he adores.'

'Lucky guy.'

'Not necessarily lucky,' she said, turning to face him. 'Maybe he and his wife don't demand as much of each other as we do...or did.'

They were so close she could feel his breath fanning her cheek. The same raw awareness that had been there on the night they'd made love was back, but she told herself they'd already been down that road once and they were still sleeping in separate beds, still wary of each other.

'So you're not happy with the way *we* are?' Piers was asking.

'Are you?' she asked, answering a question with a question and then wishing she hadn't, as she'd just given him an opening to tell her something that she might not like...

'I've accepted what we have, if that's what you mean,' he told her. 'In fact, I've had to accept a lot of things since I came back. For instance, the sad knowledge that I've lost my dad, and on the up side that I have a beautiful daughter, and way back down again the fact that you'd been managing very well without me. *That* hurt. I have my pride. Too much of it, I'm afraid. So maybe I'm not as envious of Dave and his wife as you are. Let's say I'm learning to be thankful for what I've got.'

There was a lump in her throat. 'Don't,' she said tearfully. 'I can't bear to see you humble. Humility doesn't sit well on your shoulders.'

His smile was grim. 'So what *do* you want of me? You accuse me of trying to control you, yet when I'm prepared to take a back seat you don't like that either.'

'Yes, I know that's how it seems,' she admitted. 'It *does* make it appear as if I don't know what I want, but it's because I'm afraid of it all going wrong again.'

'And you think *I'm* not?'

She sighed. 'We had such confidence in that other life, didn't we, Piers? We were on top of the world, but somehow it all went wrong.'

'Yes, it did,' he agreed. 'My pride and your stubbornness, with a dash of stupidity thrown in, made a destructive concoction.'

'You've just said that it hurt when you came back to find me managing so well. Surely you see that I had no choice,' she told him. 'You'd left me out on a limb with a child to support. No forwarding address.

Nothing! I was bitter and angry that you'd spoiled what should have been one of the happiest events in our lives.'

'I paid the price, though, didn't I? By missing out on almost two years of my daughter's life. But we're harking back to the past instead of thinking about the future. Where do we go from here, Kerry? Have we done too much damage for us ever to be able to put it right again?'

'I don't know. I just don't know,' she told him.

This was the moment to suggest that they make a fresh start by retaking their wedding vows, Piers was thinking, but as he took her hand in his the phone rang and Kerry got to her feet.

'Ignore it,' he said, and she sat down again. But whoever the caller was, they were not going to ring off and she sighed. 'We'd better answer it, Piers. It could be something important.'

Not as important as what he had been about to suggest, he thought as he picked up the receiver.

It was Natalie, phoning from the refuge to say that half the people who'd turned up for the night were sick and they couldn't get hold of a GP or an emergency doctor.

'I'll be there as fast as I can,' he told her.

'That was the refuge,' he said flatly as he put the phone down. 'An emergency. I'm going to have to go round there.'

She smiled. 'Go, then. Our affairs can wait. *We* haven't a crisis on our hands.'

'No. Just a long-term catastrophe,' he said irritably in his frustration at having the moment taken from them, and went to get his car keys.

By the time he'd got to the refuge he'd calmed down, and told himself that maybe he'd been prevented from making a fool of himself. Kerry hadn't seemed to mind him being called away in the middle of such an important discussion, and if she'd said no to taking their vows again his pride would have taken another hammering in the knowledge that she still hadn't forgiven him for what he'd done.

There was a nip in the air in the days that followed. Winter had arrived. Crisp days were sandwiched between cold dawns and dusks, and the leaves that had graced the trees in the city's parks and gardens now lay in gold and copper carpets as far as the eye could see.

It would be Rosalie's second birthday in a few days' time and whenever the occasion came around Kerry knew she would never forget the mixture of joy and misery that had been hers when their daughter was born.

One morning as they were having breakfast she said out of the blue, 'If we have a boy, I'd like him to be called Daniel after your father, if that's all right with you.'

Piers looked at her with surprised dark eyes. 'Well, yes, of course it's all right. I certainly wasn't expecting you to want him called after me, but what brought that thought to mind?'

'Because Rosalie's birthday is coming up and he was with me at that time, and for ever afterwards, until…'

'Yes. I know,' he said stiffly, 'No need to remind me.' And Kerry knew she'd hit a nerve again.

'Why would you think I wouldn't want the baby to be called after you?' she questioned, knowing that she was probably going to make matters worse.

'Because of my track record perhaps?'

'That's ridiculous,' she protested. 'Do you honestly think I would be so petty?'

He didn't give a straight answer, just shrugged and said tonelessly, '*I* might be if the boot was on the other foot.'

'No, you wouldn't,' she said softly, tuning in to his mood. 'Stop wallowing in self-criticism, Piers. You said the other night that you've accepted our life together for what it is, and I suppose it *is* better than what a lot of people have. At least we've salvaged something out of the mess we made.' She kissed him fleetingly on the cheek.

To her surprise he reached out for her and took her in his arms, and as he looked down at her, pressed up close against him, it was there, the desire that was so rare in their new life together.

His eyes were warming, his mouth close to hers, when the child inside her moved and he became still.

'I felt it,' he said wonderingly. 'I felt the baby move!'

Kerry was laughing. 'He or she wants to get in on the act,' she told him.

As Rosalie began tugging at her skirts he said with a wry smile, 'Do you get the feeling that it's a bit crowded round here?' Releasing her from his hold, he bent and picked up his daughter.

Once Lizzie had arrived they went out to their cars, ready to face whatever the day held for them at the hospital, and as Kerry watched him drive off she thought wistfully that Piers was still the most attractive man she'd ever seen.

There was a sort of lean magnetism about him that made other men seem nondescript and she knew there would never be anyone else in her life if he ever left her again.

But he wouldn't, would he? Not now she'd given him children. He adored Rosalie and would be the same with their second child when it arrived. With regard to herself he seemed to change from one moment to the next, from being withdrawn to being approachable, unmoved by her presence, to being so aware of her she could feel it coming over like the heat of a fire as it had been for those few tender moments in the kitchen earlier.

But none of it was getting them anywhere fast, and if today was like every other day, they would fulfil their functions on the trauma unit and then come home to an uneventful evening. Not exactly a magical recipe for life, but safe enough if she wanted to be safe.

As he drove through the morning rush-hour Piers's mind was on a far more positive track. He still hadn't given up on the idea of suggesting to Kerry that they take their marriage vows again, even though there was the chance that she might refuse. Yet he knew deep down that she *had* kept herself only to him and prayed she would do so until death did them part. And as for himself, he would never betray her.

She might sometimes think him cold, disdainful and doubting, but he had his code of honour. That was why he'd gone berserk when he'd thought that *she* hadn't lived up to it.

The suggestion that they take their vows again would need a ring to go with it, he thought, and decided that at the first opportunity he would stop off at a jeweller's.

At present she was his wife in name only, but maybe one day soon that would change and she would forgive him for what he'd done.

When they were on the point of leaving the hospital that evening Kerry said, 'We need to sort out what we're getting Rosalie for her birthday. Do you fancy doing a detour by the big toy shop in the shopping centre?'

'Tomorrow maybe,' he said quickly. 'I have an errand of my own to do today.'

He was hoping that she wouldn't ask him where and she didn't, which pleased and irritated him at the same time. If *she* had said the same thing, he would have wanted to know where she was going, especially in her present state. But that was because everything she did was of interest to him, while it would seem that his movements were unlikely to arouse any curiosity in her.

'I'll go myself, then, and report back,' she said. 'but we must sort it tomorrow.'

He nodded and she saw that he was smiling a secret smile, which made her wonder what he was up to.

'Sure thing,' he said. 'I wasn't there when she was one, but I'm going to make up for it this time.'

Kerry glanced at him quickly, but the smile was still there, so it would seem there had been no barb in the comment.

As he drove to the jeweller's Piers was thinking that it was fortunate that it wasn't on the same parade of shops as the toy store. Yet it wasn't far away and he would have to make sure that Kerry didn't see him there or she just might begin to get curious after all.

The eternity ring he chose was a beautiful circle of pearls and diamonds, and as he looked down at it sombrely he wondered if he would ever see it on her finger. 'Eternity' was a word that spoke for itself…for ever, endlessly. Were they capable of that sort of commitment?

When he came out of the shop he saw her in the distance, strolling along amongst the homeward-bound crowds, and he quickened his step to get away from the vicinity of the jeweller's.

She'd seen him and waved, and as they walked to meet each other it was as if no one else existed. That the crowded pavements and the noise of the traffic were somewhere else. All that mattered was that they should begin to sort out their lives, and the ring in the small velvet box in his pocket was the first step as far as he was concerned.

But his pride had already put the blight on their lives once. Would he be able to swallow it this time if Kerry didn't want to trust him again?

They went together to buy Rosalie's birthday presents the next day, taking a short break in the middle of the morning when the toy shop would be quieter than in the evening.

'I've ordered a birthday cake,' Kerry had said at the breakfast table.

'Good,' he'd commented, 'and I haven't forgotten we're going shopping.'

Rosalie was too young for a party but as her birth-day was on a Saturday Lizzie was coming round for tea, and while they waited at the checkout to pay for what they'd bought, Kerry was thinking how different their child's second birthday was going to be from her first. Piers would be there this time, filling the gap that had been so noticeable the year before, with his love for his daughter.

It was in the late afternoon that the peace between them was shattered when the nurse who'd caused con-cern some weeks earlier by mislaying a pair of sur-gical scissors was seen by Piers to be unsteady on her feet. They were on the point of operating on a man who'd crashed his car when he'd fallen asleep at the wheel and Kerry, who had also noticed the other nurse's unsteadiness, found herself tensing as Piers went across to her.

'Have you been drinking?' he asked levelly.

'No. Why?' she asked.

'Because you are swaying somewhat.'

She began to weep.

'Yes, I have had a few drinks,' she admitted. 'My husband left me this morning and I thought it might steady my nerves.'

'I see. And what about the nerves of the patient we are about to operate on? What sort of a state do you think his nerves would be in if he knew that one of my team was under the influence? Go home and don't come back until you are in a fit condition.'

'I can't do that,' she protested tearfully. 'I need the money.'

'And I need people around me that I can trust,' Piers told her inflexibly.

Kerry cringed. It was Danny Cosgrove all over again. Though in this instance Piers had just cause to be angry. But didn't he realise that the woman he'd sent home was in the same position that she'd been in once? Her husband had left her and she was in shock.

'Did you *have* to do that?' she asked in a low voice when she'd gone. 'Taking her to task in front of everyone. I know she was in the wrong, but the poor girl is demoralised.'

'She could have rung in sick.'

'I'm glad you weren't the doctor in charge when *I* had to go in to work after *you* left me,' she said angrily. 'By all means, send her home, but what about a bit of sympathy?'

He ignored the last part of what she'd said and commented dryly, 'But you wouldn't have been on the bottle, would you?'

'No! Of course not. But I was pretty low, not functioning too well, and a kind word meant a lot.'

'Then they should have sent you home, too, if you weren't up to it.'

'You have some nerve to be passing comment on what I or *they* should have done when you'd been the cause of it,' she flared back. 'And do we *have* to brawl in public?'

'Who started it?' he said. 'Not me. I am responsible for the safety of the injured who are brought to us, Kerry, and if you think that history is repeating itself, I can't help that. So once the anaesthetist is ready for us, we'll get on with the job, shall we?'

Having said all she had to say, she nodded, and within minutes all but the accident victim on the table was banished from her mind.

When it was time to finish at the end of the day Piers was the first to leave as the nurses had more cleaning up to do, with one of them being missing, but it didn't stop Kerry from paying a call on the deserted wife, Emma, on her way home.

'I'm all right,' she said when she opened the door to her. 'I was a fool to turn up in that state, but I had no idea that Jack intended leaving me and I wasn't thinking straight this morning. We've been having problems but nothing so serious as to call for that. Or at least so I thought.'

Kerry knew that she had two little girls and she asked, 'Where are Becky and Amy?'

'At my parents' house. They don't know what's happened yet and I'm not looking forward to telling them.'

As Kerry nodded sympathetically, the stricken woman picked up an envelope off the table and asked, 'Do you know anything about this?'

'Why, what is it?' she asked.

'It's a cheque from Mr Jefferson with a note to say it's to cover any earnings I might have lost today, and it's far more than it needs to be. It was on the mat when I went into the hall a few moments ago.'

As Kerry looked down on to Piers's bold scrawl there was a lump in her throat. Had he done this because of what she'd said, she wondered, or simply because he was Piers Jefferson, the enigma that she'd married, who had once left *her* high and dry?

'You're late,' he said when she arrived home.

A SURGEON'S MARRIAGE WISH

'Yes, I know. I called to see Emma, the nurse that you sent off the unit.'

'Oh, I see. And how is she now?'

He wasn't meeting her glance and Kerry thought he was wondering if she knew about the cheque.

'Much better, now that she doesn't have to worry about money for a little while.'

'So she told you?'

'About the cheque, yes. I'm sorry I said my piece about you sending her home. I thought you didn't care about what happened to her.'

'You mean like the way I didn't care when I did the same thing to you? I expected you to understand that the patient comes before anyone's personal problems, and I wasn't prepared to let her near him in the state she was in, but it didn't mean that I didn't care about what had happened to her. I'm still on a guilt trip over what I did to you and thought that the money might help a bit.'

He'd been peeling potatoes and when he turned back to continue his task Kerry's glance was on the way the thick, dark pelt of his hair was shaped into his neck and the hands that had exchanged a scalpel for a potato peeler. Piers was a mixture of many things, she thought, and not more so than today.

As Piers helped Rosalie to unwrap her presents on her birthday Kerry felt that it was as if their lives were made up of peaks and valleys, that they never seemed to be on the level ground.

Today they were up amongst the peaks because it was Rosalie's birthday. But only the other day they'd been down in the valley when she'd thought that there was going to be another episode like Piers's treatment of Danny Cosgrove. Until he'd shown practical concern for the desolate nurse.

Some might envy them, think they were a striking couple from the outside, doing a vital job, with a beautiful child, yet there were times when Kerry longed for the sameness of everyday life, to know that she and Piers were on the same wavelength, instead of always having to brace herself against the next conflict of minds.

But she'd already decided that today was going to be Rosalie's day with not a cloud in the sky. When Lizzie arrived in the late afternoon no one would have known that she and Piers weren't the perfect parents, but, then, they were, none better. It was the husband-and-wife part that they still had to get sorted.

While he was playing with the birthday girl Lizzie wandered into the kitchen.

'Are things any better with Piers?' she asked in a low voice.

'Yes, I think they are a little, but we're still groping our way through the fog, trying to understand what each other is thinking, and it isn't easy where he is concerned. I still feel that he sees me more as the provider of his children than the love of his life. I was that once, but not any more.'

'I can't believe that,' Lizzie protested.

'I'm afraid that you might have to,' Kerry told her.

On a grey December afternoon the team were fighting to save the life of a fireman in his fifties who had been hit by falling masonry at a big factory fire in Lambeth.

His helmet had saved his head, but the stone slab that had hit him had caused severe damage to his arms and chest and he'd been brought in on a backboard as there seemed to be no sensation in his legs.

There had been no pulse or heartbeat when the helicopter had swooped down from the sky to pick him up and the doctor on board had thought they'd lost him. But urgent resuscitation had triumphed and the man had started to breathe again.

And now his injuries were being treated, while outside in the corridor his son, also a member of the fire service, was going through the agony of waiting to hear if his father was going to live, knowing that though the fire was still raging their participation in tackling the blaze was over, with the older man fighting for his life. He had fractures of the forearms, a crushed chest and, even more serious, X-rays had shown a dislocation of the spine that was causing paralysis of the lower limbs.

'We're going to have to wire the fractured bone ends to stabilise them,' the orthopaedic surgeon on the team said. 'This guy isn't going to be fighting fires for some months to come.'

Piers nodded his agreement. Once again they would be dealing with the most serious injuries first and putting on hold the ones that could wait for a short time. He glanced across at Kerry who was arranging the instruments that were going to be needed and said in a low voice, 'You'll soon be away from all this, sitting with your feet up awaiting the arrival of Jefferson child number two.'

'You can't wait to get me away from here, can you?' she said wearily, and his face closed up.

Her legs were aching. She'd been on her feet for hours, and she was gasping for a cup of tea, but she wasn't going to tell Piers that. She had every intention of finishing work in the new year, and if they'd been communicating as they should have been she would have discussed it with him. As it was, she had decided that at seven months pregnant, which would take her past Christmas, she would bow out of the trauma unit gracefully and didn't need any reminders.

He'd turned away and was discussing the surgery that was about to take place on the injured firefighter. She couldn't see his expression, but his jawline had tightened and she wondered why she'd been so quick to see his concern as interference.

It had been there again, Piers thought glumly as he drove home that night. The feeling that Kerry thought all he cared about were his children. It was because she'd looked pale and tired that he'd said what he had. She was as precious to him as they were. That was why he'd been so unreasonable and jealous all that time ago, but he hadn't found the right words then and it was the same now.

Would Kerry want Lizzie to mind the new baby when her maternity leave was up? he wondered as his thoughts switched to another matter not yet discussed. He couldn't think of anyone better to do so if his wife wanted to continue her career, but he was prepared to wait until Kerry brought the subject up, especially after her reaction to his comment about her finishing work in the near future.

Working with her had always been a joy and it was no different now. She was quick and knowledgable and read his mind when they were on opposite sides of the operating table, but sadly she didn't pick up on his thoughts as quickly when they were away from it.

A florist not far from where they lived was getting ready to close for the day and he stopped the car and whipped in smartly. He couldn't remember the last time he'd bought her flowers, and as the assistant made up a bouquet of pale cream roses and lily of the valley his heart was beating faster.

He wanted her to know that he was sorry for making it seem as if he was pushing her out of the job she loved before she was ready. If she would give him the chance he would explain that it was because he cared about her well-being that he'd said what he had.

They usually arrived home about the same time, but tonight Lizzie's car had gone and he could see Kerry in the kitchen, preparing the evening meal.

Her eyes widened when she saw the flowers but she didn't speak, just stared at him with a big wooden spoon in her hand while Rosalie played beside her.

'These are for you,' he said quietly.

'Why?' she wanted to know.

'Maybe because I always think of you when I see cream roses. Then again it might be because I'm sorry for making it sound as if I'm trying to push you out of the unit to suit my own ends. I said what I did because you looked pale and tired and I was concerned for you. Obviously you will make your own decision regarding when you're going to finish.'

She had changed into a long stretchy skirt and a cotton top and, having taken the flowers from his outstretched hand, was holding them carefully.

Tears were threatening but she blinked them back. Moments like this were so rare between them she couldn't believe it was happening.

'I would prefer the date of my departure from the unit to be our joint decision, Piers,' she told him, 'but since the night you were called out to the refuge, when we were having a heart to heart, we've never had another serious talk.'

'For a very good reason,' he responded dryly. 'When I *do* have anything to say I only seem to make matters worse.'

'Not always,' she said with a smile. 'And now, if I can find a vase to equal the magnificence of the roses, I'll put them in water.'

CHAPTER EIGHT

As THEY dined that dark December night, with Rosalie sleeping above, Kerry's glance kept going to the flowers and she wondered if Piers had any idea how much pleasure it gave her, knowing they were from him, and also knowing that he'd remembered that she'd carried cream roses and lily of the valley on their wedding day.

But, then, he would, wouldn't he, she thought. Piers had a memory second to none. Maybe that was what had kept him away for so long. Memories of his wife in another man's arms. Yet he had come back. Swallowed his pride and come in out of the cold. Though not back to *her* in the first instance, and that hurt. It was at the root of the uncertainty that always lay below the surface of her mind.

He'd never admitted anything other than he'd come back because of the job that he'd been offered. Then he'd discovered he had a child and now nothing would make him budge. He was here to stay because of Rosalie. But tonight for the first time since his return she felt as if *she* mattered, and it was all because of a bouquet.

They took their coffee into the sitting room and when they were settled in front of the fire Kerry said, 'What do you think about me finishing work at the end of January?'

'It's fine by me,' he told her, keen to dispel any

148

chance of being seen as a dictator. 'Just as long as you feel up to carrying on until then.'

'So we have agreement on that,' she said, as if she hadn't been expecting it.

He was frowning. 'We do indeed, and there's no need to sound so surprised. As you know, I don't like important issues left up in the air. What did you expect me to do, start laying down the law? Insisting that you finish sooner than that? If there's one thing I've learnt in recent months, it is to be patient,' he told her, and thought of the ring, hidden beneath papers in the desk drawer in the study. 'And as you know, patience is something that has always been in short supply where I'm concerned.'

She smiled. 'Yes. I *do* know that, but you've changed, Piers. We both have. Maybe we needed to be jolted out of our brash over-confidence, and if we've come out of it less selfish and more tolerant maybe it was worth all the pain. I want us to be an ordinary family, like that of Dave, the taxi driver. He told me that he and his wife had never spent a night apart since they got married until he was involved in that terrible accident, and it made me think that it was something that *we* couldn't boast of.'

'Our burly friend really did make an impression on you, didn't he?' he remarked dryly. 'He called in the other day after he'd been to Outpatients and was disappointed that you weren't there. I explained that you only worked certain days and we had a brief chat. He's making good progress and hopes to be back on the road soon. But first he'll have to prove to the authorities that he's really fit. They won't let just anyone drive a taxi.

'Getting back to what you said about his domestic bliss, I suppose you're right. *We've* spent more nights apart than we've been together and have only ourselves to blame for that.'

'And what do you suggest we do about it?' she asked. 'For my part, I need to feel that you trust me. That if another Danny Cosgrove came on the scene you would see it as it was, me looking after the vulnerable, not having a rampant affair.'

'I think I could manage that,' he said stiffly, loath to admit that he might have used the Cosgrove affair to cover up how much he'd been smarting at the way their marriage had been breaking up.

'I know that you want me in a physical sense,' Kerry said. 'Sometimes being near you is like being near fire. You have only to touch me and I melt. But at others it's like being out in the cold and the contrast is too much to cope with.

'But we could go on like this for ever, raking over old coals. So getting back to those things that you'd like to see settled, tomorrow I'll inform Personnel that I'm finishing at the end of January. I'm going for an antenatal check-up first thing, but I'll speak to them as soon as that's over.'

'Are you keeping a close watch on your blood pressure?'

'Need you ask? Yes, I am. I check it each day and so far it's fine. You're not the only one who hasn't forgotten the scare we had in the early stages.'

'Which *you* were inclined to make light of.'

She shook her head. 'That's not true. You were uptight and abrupt when all I wanted was for you to hold me and tell me it was going to be all right, and because you weren't doing that it made me want to play it down. You didn't read my mind.'

'So is there any chance that I'm reading your mind right now and that you want to share my bed tonight?' he asked, knowing that he was going back on all his resolves.

'That thought is in my mind every night of my life, Piers, but I try to ignore it. Knowing, as you were quick to point out, that making love as we did that time was the wrong way round. There should have been love and trust between us first, and until we can say we have that, let's keep to our separate bedrooms.'

'Sure, if that's how you feel,' he said equably, wishing he'd never made the suggestion, while Kerry, annoyed by his easy acceptance of her refusal, wondered what was going on in his mind.

Piers got to his feet and, looking down at her, he said, 'I've some household accounts to sort out. I'll see you in the morning.'

He cursed softly into the empty study as he closed the door behind him. Whatever had possessed him to try to push matters along at the risk of a rebuff? But Kerry, sitting opposite him with the lamplight turning her hair to gold, had looked so beautiful that he'd given in to the ache inside him, thrown caution to the winds and asked her to sleep with him. And a lot of good it had done him!

He went across to the desk and fished out the ring from its hiding place. As he looked down at it lying on the palm of his hand, he thought sombrely that the day he brought it out into the open would be the most important day of his life. There would be no turning back. He would be committed for ever more, and if she refused it he would have nowhere left to go.

With Christmas approaching fast Kerry wondered constantly what it was going to be like. They'd spent the last two apart and there'd been little joy in them without Piers. Daniel had been there for her, kind and supportive as always, but it was her husband that she'd yearned for and now he was here, the best Christmas gift she could have ever asked for, but was what was inside the wrapping what she wanted?

Life on the unit was becoming more hectic with each passing day as the festive season drew nearer. The heightened activity of a capital city moving towards Christmas and the frenetic festivities it brought with it were bringing more accidents than usual to A and E.

The week before Christmas the surgeon in charge of the night team fell ill and Piers was asked to take over. Because of the time of year, those on night shift were under most pressure and they couldn't risk being one short when casualties were being brought in constantly by helicopter or the ambulances working with the unit's fast-response vehicles.

He had agreed to fill the gap. The need was there. It was as simple as that. Also, he'd decided that working through the night hours he would be away from the thought that had him tossing and turning, Kerry asleep just across the landing.

When he'd told her he was going to be in charge of the night shift for a while she'd nodded understandingly. Only someone working on the trauma unit

knew the pressures and the expertise that were required to treat those that were brought to them.

Yet it didn't stop her from wishing it hadn't happened. They might sleep in separate beds, but she'd
grown used to knowing that Piers was nearby during
the night hours, and with her pregnancy well on the
way to its conclusion she was glad of his presence
more than ever.

Whether he had similar feelings she didn't know.
It hadn't been easy for him since he'd come back into
her life. First of all, he'd had to face up to the loss
of his father, followed by their uneasy alliance. Living
together with memories of the hurtful past always in
their minds. Plus a pregnancy that they both wanted,
but maybe not for the right reasons. And interwoven
amongst all of that was her refusal to sleep with him.
So perhaps he would be glad of a change of scene.
Out of her orbit at night and asleep during the day.

In the meantime, there was Christmas to think
about, with the possibility that he might be working
as festive holidays for the public meant less time off
for medical staff.

They'd been invited to Lizzie's for Christmas Day
lunch and her friend had teased, 'I'm going to get a
huge bunch of mistletoe and manoeuvre the two of
you beneath it.'

'I wouldn't be too hopeful.' Kerry had told her.
'Piers asked me to sleep with him not so long ago
and I refused. Don't ask me why. I must have been
insane. But it was all so cold-blooded and he didn't
appear the least bit upset when I said no. It was as if
he was testing me. Now he's working nights and I

feel that he's glad of the opportunity to put some space between us.'

'I don't believe that for one moment,' Lizzie declared. 'The man is in love with you. Why don't you make the opportunity for him to tell you so, instead of keeping him at arm's length? Make yourself so desirable that he can't resist you.'

Kerry's smile was wry. 'I'm nearly seven months pregnant and bulging out all over. And we are talking about Piers Jefferson, man of iron, who cast his wife to one side on a mere suspicion. He's with me now because of Rosalie and the child I'm carrying. We're not exactly galloping towards a big reconciliation.'

Lizzie sighed. 'What do you think is going to happen when the new baby comes?'

'I don't know,' Kerry told her. 'I just don't know. We'll probably carry on as we are, with Piers revelling in his children and tolerating his wife. Remember, Lizzie, he didn't come back to London for me. He came back to his roots because of the job he'd been offered.'

I'll be working Christmas Eve and Boxing Day night,' Piers told her, 'and for the rest of the time I'll be home.'

She was in the middle of making mince pies when he'd come home in the morning with weariness upon him after a busy night, and he arrived just as the first batch was coming out of the oven. As he helped himself to one of the hot pastries, he smiled across at her and said, 'So are we all geared up for Christmas?'

Kerry smiled back. 'Yes, and if you're going to be working part of it we'll have to make the best of the times that you aren't. What did you do at Christmas when you were in New Zealand?'

The smile disappeared and she thought that it had been tactless to ask such a question, but surely he hadn't moped all the time. He was too much of a livewire.

'I worked,' he said abruptly. 'What did *you* do while I was away?'

'Looked after Rosalie and did the best I could,' she replied. 'The first Christmas she was only a few weeks old. It was then that Daniel came looking for me and suggested that I move in here with him, and because I was lonely and miserable I agreed.'

'Better the father than the son when it came to looking after you, it would seem,' he said flatly, and she wondered why she had asked the question. Every time they were in a relaxed mood she spoilt it for one reason or another, and she'd just done it again.

'You weren't to know we had a child,' she said softly.

'True,' he said in the same monotone, 'and as we seem to have gone over that scenario a few times, I'll leave you to your baking and try to get some sleep.'

As Piers was leaving for the hospital on Christmas Eve he said, 'I'll be home as soon as I can in the morning. You won't let Rosalie open her presents until I arrive, will you?'

'Of course I won't!' Kerry exclaimed indignantly. 'If I hadn't booked some leave for this week, it might have been me dashing home on Christmas morning instead of you...or both of us.'

He smiled. 'OK. Sorry. But it *is* my first Christmas with her.'

'I know,' she said equably. 'I hope that you're prepared for a much quieter occasion than our Christmases used to be when we were partying from morning until night the moment we came off duty.'

'I *am* prepared,' he said levelly. 'One's values change with circumstances. In the last few months mine have had a complete overhaul.'

Kerry could feel her heart beating faster. It was turning out to be one of their rare moments of understanding, but the clock was ticking on. He hadn't the time to linger, and so she pinned her hopes on the following morning, Christmas Day, when he would be back with them.

Once Piers had gone she took out the gifts she had for him and began to wrap them. One was a photograph of his father that he'd never seen. It had been taken at a dinner that Daniel had presided over on behalf of the hospital trust and had been passed to her by the director with the comment, 'I'll leave it to you to give it to Piers. You'll know when the time is right.'

Silver-haired and genial, in evening dress for the occasion, it was an astounding likeness and she'd had it framed with the style and taste that she knew would appeal to his son.

Along with the photograph there was a watch to wrap and a stylish silk dressing-gown of oriental design. She'd bought some gift wrap the previous day and placed it in the desk drawer, and as she rummaged around for the labels that went with it her hand closed around a small velvet box.

Curiosity had her bringing it out from under the paperwork where it had been lying, and when she lifted the lid and saw the circle of diamonds and pearls she gasped.

Piers had bought her a ring for Christmas! Not just any sort of a band to go on her finger, but an eternity ring. A symbol of continuing love between two people. They were almost there. He did really love her after all.

It was Christmas morning and when Piers came striding into the kitchen at eight o'clock to find his wife and daughter waiting for him and a special Christmas breakfast ready to be eaten, the traumas of a Christmas Eve that had mostly been alcohol-related began to fade into the background.

He was happy, happier than he'd been for ages, and it was due to these two, he thought. His golden-haired wife, big and beautiful in her pregnancy, and his daughter, dark-eyed, dark-haired like himself.

It was like coming home to a haven of peace after being embroiled in the pain and troubles of others for twelve hours. He was exhausted but the tiredness was falling off him and as he opened their gifts to him there was a new feeling of belonging inside him.

His eyes were moist as he looked at the photograph of his father, and as he fastened the watch onto the wrist that she'd seen wielding a scalpel a thousand times there was a pleased smile on his face. It was the same when he tried on the robe and Kerry teased, 'You look like the King of Siam, but I'm hardly the right shape for the governess.'

'And I'm not going to shave my head,' he told her

laughingly. Still wearing the kingly robe, he went into the study and came back with his arms full of packages.

Her eyes were bright with anticipation but it faded when she saw that there was no small box amongst them, unless it was included with something else, yet she knew that it couldn't be as it had been lying unwrapped at the bottom of the drawer when she'd seen it the night before.

There was a book by a top women's writer that she'd said she would like to read, an expensive leather handbag, perfume, a necklace that glittered up at her mockingly from a pad of black velvet, but no ring.

He'd seen her expression and asked, 'What's wrong? Haven't I hit the right note?'

With disappointment dragging at her, she dredged up a smile. The ring could have been there ever since he'd come back from New Zealand, she thought. It might have nothing to do with her.

'No, everything is lovely,' she said with false enthusiasm. 'And now are we going to have breakfast?'

'You bet,' he agreed, determined not to let her see that he knew he'd boobed but wasn't sure how. Maybe she thought he was presuming too much, buying her gifts, but he'd made sure they were nothing too personal and *she* had bought presents for him.

He would have liked to have given Kerry lingerie, beautiful satin underwear that would be waiting for her when she'd had the baby. Or more than anything the ring, lying unused and unpresented at the bottom of the desk drawer.

But he was sticking to his intention. He had to be sure that when he gave it to her, Kerry would accept it. There was no way he would be able to carry on with his self-imposed celibacy if she didn't, and her reaction to his gifts wasn't encouraging.

He observed that she perked up when they arrived at Lizzie's for Christmas lunch and wished, as he had before, that Kerry was as relaxed with him as she was with her friends.

With Rosalie between them, they stood in the doorway of the dining room when it was time to eat and the mistletoe was directly overhead. Piers saw it and smiled, and as Kerry eyed him expectantly he bent and kissed their daughter.

'So much for romance under the mistletoe,' she said wryly when the two women found themselves alone in the kitchen at the end of the meal. 'Anyone would think I had something catching.'

Lizzie sighed sympathetically.

'Yes, but at least Piers kissed one of the women in his life.'

'Hmm. Maybe there are others.'

'You are joking!' her friend said.

'There's a beautiful eternity ring hidden in the desk drawer.'

'And?'

'I thought it might be for me, but it wasn't among my presents this morning.'

'So what? Have you a birthday coming up, or a special anniversary?'

'No, neither.'

'So just remember what we have always said about him. That Piers is rock solid in spite of your differences. That he would never look at another woman.'

'And are we that smart that we've never been wrong?' Kerry retorted.

In spite of the promise of Christmas morning not materialising, the day turned out to be a happy one, with Kerry reminding herself that at least they were together, ring or no ring, and maybe Lizzie *was* right about him being a one-woman man, though it was taking him a long time to get around to telling her so if he was.

His joke about the tattoo came back to mind. *Had* he once slept with a woman who had a tattoo? Bought the ring for her and then had a rethink?

In the late afternoon, in the middle of a complicated board game that Lizzie had bought, Piers leaned back in his seat and let the previous night's exertions catch up with him. Looking down at him as he slept, Kerry wondered if it mattered about the ring hidden in the drawer. He came home each night to her and Rosalie and was going to continue to do so, and that was all that mattered.

But it wasn't, of course. What mattered was that she loved him deeply and not by word or deed since they'd been back together had he ever hinted that he felt the same about her.

He was kind and caring, generous with his time and energy, but after that time when he'd asked if she would sleep with him and she'd refused, Piers had never turned towards her bedroom door on the nights when he wasn't working.

And now January had arrived, with winter's cold bringing frosty nights and mornings to the city and winds that nipped at the ankles and noses of those going about their business on its streets.

The sales were on in full force for those who had preferred to wait for a bargain in January rather than something gift-wrapped on Christmas morning, or maybe had cash left over from the expenses of the festive season, or were just simply shopaholics.

Piers was now back on the day shift. The surgeon who'd been ill had recovered and Kerry was glad to have her husband's presence in the house once more during the long dark nights, and in the daytime where she was used to seeing him, at the other side of the operating table.

On the Friday of the last week of the month Kerry had more important things than the sales on her mind. It was her last day on the unit, the last day she would be working with Piers and the rest of the team.

She was loath to leave yet ready to go. Being on her feet all day and then going home to prepare a meal was becoming more of a chore than a pleasure. Even though Piers cleared away afterwards and then put Rosalie to bed, she was nearly always asleep in front of the fire when he came down again.

That he would have liked her to finish earlier she had no doubt, but he'd agreed with her suggestion when she should leave the unit and hadn't gone back on his word. He also hadn't asked any questions about whether she would want to go back to work once the baby was old enough to be left, and if he had she wouldn't have known what to tell him.

Lizzie had told her that she would look after the new arrival as well as Rosalie if she wanted to go back to work, and there was no one other than her friend that Kerry would trust with such a responsibility. But Lizzie wouldn't be available for ever, Kerry kept telling herself.

She might get married and want babies of her own one day. Added to that, she knew that Piers wanted her to be a full-time mother to his children and it was what *she* wanted, too. Yet working in the busiest A and E department for miles around gave her a lot of job satisfaction and experienced theatre nurses didn't grow on trees.

But as the day progressed she put those sort of thoughts to the back of her mind. Some of those who weren't on duty or had families to see to were taking her out for a farewell meal. They would be making their way there at the end of the shift, but Piers wouldn't be with them as he would be going home to relieve Lizzie.

She would much rather have spent a quiet evening with him but felt it would have been ungracious not to fall in with the suggestion of a meal at a restaurant not far from the hospital that the staff always went to on such occasions.

The food was good, the drinks flowing, and Kerry thought that everyone was in high spirits except her, sipping on a tonic water. It didn't help when one of the nurses said jokingly, 'Cheer up. There isn't one of us who wouldn't jump at the chance of getting away from all the blood and broken bones to play happy families with Piers Jefferson.'

In that moment the futility of her life with Piers hit her like a physical blow, but she managed a smile. These were her friends. They all had their ups and downs on the marital merry-go-round, but she didn't think any of them were living a lie like Piers and herself…the perfect couple who'd turned out to be not so perfect after all.

Piers had waited up for her and instead of being pleased Kerry wished she could have just gone to bed without having to discuss the evening's events. She wasn't to know that he was fully aware of her mixed feelings about leaving the unit and understood. But he also thought that as there was such an important reason for her doing so, surely she wouldn't hold that against him, too.

'So how did it go?' he said easily, as if unaware of her mood.

'Fine,' she replied flatly. 'Until someone remarked how lucky I was to be playing happy families with you.'

'And you didn't like that.'

'I might have done if it was true.'

'You mean that you don't think you *are* lucky?' He was still speaking in the same easy tone and she couldn't bear it.

'Let's say that there are varying degrees of being lucky.'

He ignored that. 'And obviously you don't think we are a happy family either.'

'Well, are we?'

'There are lots worse.'

'So you're prepared for us to go on like this!' she cried, with the thought of the ring in the drawer still gnawing at her. She was tempted to challenge him over it, but if it had nothing to do with her it would be just too humiliating.

'If I have to…yes,' he said steadily. 'I'm here to support my family. Trying to make up for the past.'

'And that's it?'

'What more do you want?' he said through gritted teeth, his earlier good humour disappearing. 'This?'

He reached out for her, took her face between his hands and kissed her, and it was not the kiss of a dutiful husband. It was a lover's kiss, bone-melting, demanding, and because she was so hungry for him Kerry kissed him back as if she wanted it to go on for ever.

But Piers had other ideas. He released her and told her flatly, 'All this is because you're upset at leaving the unit, isn't it? You are blaming me for it. Lots of women would be thrilled to be in your position and only too ready to take it easy for the last weeks of their pregnancy, but not you. And it's all because of the way this child of ours was conceived, isn't it?'

She stared at him aghast. So Piers thought that she regretted that night when their hunger for each other had cast aside every other thought. She could remember Lizzie asking what it had felt like and she'd said that it had been wonderful, like nothing she'd ever known before, and here he was, making it seem like something not very nice.

'I'm going to bed,' she said bleakly, 'but before I do I think you need to know that I don't blame you for anything that you've done since you came back into my life. Our problems go further back than that, or have you forgotten? And I *am* looking forward to having the baby. I can't believe you should think otherwise. I was stupid to let a joking remark get to me like it did, but it does show that we aren't exactly the blissful couple that others think we are.'

She hesitated for a moment, hoping that Piers would say something to make things right, but he just gave her a long level look and began to climb the stairs.

Once inside his bedroom he threw himself onto the bed and gave a long shuddering sigh. It would have been so easy to bring Kerry up here with him after that earth-moving kiss. Their hunger for each other had been there again, but it would have been another occasion when desire had been triggered by a dispute and he didn't want a repeat of that. So he'd ended it and once again he had made matters worse.

CHAPTER NINE

ACROSS the landing Kerry was peeling off her clothes and thinking miserably that she'd picked a row, taken out her depression on Piers instead of keeping it to herself. She could still feel his mouth on hers. Her blood was still warm with the longing it had created.

Nothing had changed regarding their desires, she thought miserably. They had only to touch and they were on fire. It was the other part of their lives that was still not right. The closeness that developed between husband and wife just wasn't there, and all because of something that had happened in the past, that had been so trivial and yet so damaging.

When she went downstairs on Saturday morning after a night of sluggish sleep, Piers was nowhere to be seen and his car had gone from the front of the house.

Panic gripped her. He wasn't due at the hospital over the weekend. Had he left her once again, unable to stand the way they were living any more? She shook her head. He'd made it clear the previous night that he was prepared to carry on as they were, and even if Piers could exist without *her*, he would never leave Rosalie.

She looked out of the window countless times for any signs of his return while she gave Rosalie her breakfast, and afterwards, while she played with her

166

toys, Kerry curled up on the sofa beside her in a miserable heap.

Bogged down by the added uncertainties that the day had brought, she closed her eyes and the first she knew of Piers's return was when she became conscious of someone bending over her. When she looked up he was there, gazing down at her with the dark intensity that never gave away his innermost thoughts.

Raising herself to a sitting position, she cried, 'Where have you been? Your bed looked as if it had been slept in, yet when I came downstairs you were nowhere to be seen. How could you go off and leave us like that without a word?'

His expression was sombre. 'After last night I didn't think I would be missed...and I *did* leave word. The phone rang at half past one in the morning. It was Natalie at the refuge, asking if I could possibly go round there. They needed a doctor and they couldn't get hold of anyone else, so I scribbled a note and left it on the hall table. I presume that it must have wafted off when I went out and that the newsboy dropped the morning paper on top of it, as I've just found it. So what was the problem, Kerry? Did you think I'd left you *again*?'

'No, of course not,' she said quickly. 'Your clothes were still in the wardrobe.'

'The idea must have crossed your mind or you wouldn't have looked,' he remarked dryly. 'You still don't trust me, do you?'

'It wasn't a matter of trust,' she protested wearily. 'Lots of people go missing for many different reasons

and they don't always pack bags. It has happened
once before, don't forget.'

'Thanks for reminding me of *that* once again…and
I wasn't missing that time.'

'Oh, no? That might be how you see it, but your
father and I didn't know where you were and that to
me is the same as missing.

'All right,' he agreed flatly. 'Have it how you will.
I'm going to have a quick bite and then I'm going to
do what I always seem to be doing these days, catch
up on some sleep.'

'What was the problem at the refuge?' Kerry enquired belatedly as he moved towards the kitchen.

'One of the guys there had acute appendicitis. It
was touch and go when they got him to hospital. He'd
been in a lot of pain but it had eased off and those at
the refuge nearly didn't send for me. They weren't
aware that with appendicitis the most dangerous time
is when the pain disappears as the appendix is about
to burst, or has already done so, and it could be fatal.'

'And that took all night?' she couldn't refrain from
asking.

'No, it didn't, but as I was there I checked out some
of the others who were verging on hypothermia and
malnutrition and made sure they got the treatment
they required. I never dreamt that you hadn't found
my note.'

'I'm sorry for screeching at you like I did, Piers,'
she said contritely. 'I sometimes forget that first and
foremost you are a doctor.'

'I am also equally a husband and father,' he said
levelly, looking up from where he was making him-

self a sandwich. 'Though I doubt that I rate as high in that part of my life as I might in Theatre.'

They were at it again, Kerry thought, going round in circles, but at that moment it didn't matter. What *did* matter was that he was home safe, back where he belonged.

On Monday morning it seemed strange not to have to rush, and once Piers had set off for the hospital Kerry sat down to read the daily paper before getting dressed. As she was leafing through it an item caught her attention.

DOCTOR RISKS LIFE TO TREAT MAN IN CLUB BRAWL it said, and as she read on her eyes widened.

It appeared that Dr. Piers Jefferson, on his way home from a visit to a patient in the early hours of Saturday morning, had witnessed a man being attacked by two others outside a club. The victim had been lying on the pavement and the doctor had stopped his car and gone to help, realising by his lack of movement that the man was either dead or unconscious.

The attackers had then turned on him and threatened him, but undeterred he had rung for an ambulance and checked that the victim was still alive and that he hadn't swallowed his tongue. He had then protected him from further assault as a silent crowd had looked on, until the police and emergency services came.

When she'd finished reading Kerry put the paper down slowly. Piers had never said anything about it when he'd been giving her an account of how he'd spent the night, she thought disbelievingly. He was something else!

She'd been on edge about his absence for purely domestic reasons. What would she have been like if she'd known about that? It was typical of him that he hadn't thought it worth mentioning. To Piers, with his calm confidence, it would have just been another occasion to use his skills to save a life. The dangerous scenario that had gone with it would have been of secondary importance.

He had sailed into a situation like that and taken over. His cool authority must have made the assailants think twice before continuing their attack on the man on the ground or transferring their brutality to his rescuer.

But supposing it hadn't worked out like that. Piers could have been injured or even killed, and then he would have been 'missing' for all time, without knowing how much she cared.

The last thing he would be expecting was that the press had picked up on it, but he would find out when she showed him the paper that evening, unless he'd already seen it.

When she heard his key in the lock Kerry went down the hall to greet him, and as soon as he was inside waved the paper under his nose.

'Just a little something you forgot to mention,' she said gravely.

She was thinking that if she had any sense she would tell him that she loved him for what he'd done. Not just for the medical help he'd once again given to those at the refuge, but for going to the aid of someone who hadn't been able to defend himself.

But all day she'd been thinking about the risk he'd taken and the agony of what life would have been like without him, so she said instead, 'You put your life at risk on Friday night, Piers. Did you stop to think about us, Rosalie and me? What we would have done if anything had happened to you?'

He was observing her with wary dark eyes. 'I was hoping that you wouldn't have seen it in the papers. The last thing I expected was for the press to have got hold of the story. But now that you know, what would you have wanted me to do, Kerry? Drive on? Look the other way? I don't think so. I did what I've been trained to do and I'm sorry that you don't approve. Maybe one day I'll get it right where you are concerned.'

'You're misunderstanding me,' she said, fighting back tears. 'I think you are brave, compassionate and tireless when it comes to those who need you, but I need you, too, Piers…and so do our children.'

His expression had softened and there was a glint in his eye. He was smiling like the Piers she had once known. For once the toned-down version that she lived with really was gone and her heart skipped a beat. Was a kind word all it needed to turn him back into the dark seducer who had swept her off her feet and married her before she'd had time to gather her wits? Then almost before the confetti had been swept up had revealed for the craziest of reasons a cold, possessive side to his character that she hadn't been able to relate to?

'A kind word!' he cried in mock amazement. 'What have I done to deserve that?'

Kerry laughed back at him. There were too many sombre times in their lives these days. But she was hoping that the night ahead wasn't going to be one of them. They were going to the theatre with tickets that had been one of her Christmas gifts to him. She had reminded him that morning that they had to eat early and that Lizzie was coming round to take care of Rosalie.

'I don't need reminding,' he'd said evasively, and she'd thought that he didn't want to go. But now that the incident outside the club had come to light she guessed it must have been because he'd had that on his mind. Her spirits were lifting. It was going to be a good night.

Their first visit to the theatre had been spoilt by the emergency callout after the explosion at the apartment block and they hadn't been out, just the two of them, since then so she was really looking forward to it.

At seven and half months pregnant it wasn't easy to find the right thing to wear, and Kerry hesitated between something loose and floaty in pale blue and a more fitting outfit of black skirt and top that would cling to her ample waistline.

She decided to ask Piers and he said, 'The black, I think. It isn't the fashion to disguise pregnancy at the moment. All the celebrities like to accentuate the fact.'

'Maybe, but I'm not one of them,' she protested. 'I'm just a theatre nurse.'

'Past tense. You are now a stay-at-home wife and mother, and you are as attractive as any of them.'

'Thanks for the reminder wrapped up in a compli-
ment,' she said, at that moment too happy to be
ruffled.

So it was the black, and when Lizzie arrived she
said, 'Wow! Someone is out to make a statement.'

'It was Piers's choice,' Kerry told her.

'I can see why,' she replied laughingly. 'Pregnant
prima donnas and stars of stage and screen, eat your
hearts out.'

The show was like the one they'd had to leave in such
haste that other time, an excellent new version of an
old favourite, and the pleasure of having Piers to herself was adding greatly to her enjoyment. Maybe if
there'd been more times like this they might have
drawn closer, she thought.

Yet it wasn't the old days now. They had Rosalie
and soon there would be another little one to care for,
and her job hadn't exactly been of the kind that left
much energy at the end of the day for hitting the high
spots.

But tonight they'd made it and as she looked at
Piers sitting beside her there was a lump in her throat.
The ring was still in the drawer, which had to mean
something, though she didn't know what. Either it
was meant for her and he wasn't falling over himself
to present it or, as she'd surmised before, maybe it
had been there all along.

Perhaps it had nothing to do with the woman with
the tattoo and had belonged to his mother. Kerry
knew that she'd died when he'd been only in his teens
and that her loss had brought father and son together
in a very close bond.

She sighed. Whatever the reason for its presence, it certainly wasn't getting the chance to see the light of day. She'd wanted to ask him what it was doing there countless times but hadn't been able to find the right words.

'A penny for them,' he said, having heard the sigh. 'Though I'm sure your thoughts are worth more than that.'

'Yes, they are,' she agreed, recalling the circle of sparkling gems. 'Much more.'

'Why don't we do this more often?' he said at the interval. 'I haven't felt so relaxed in ages.'

'That's because we're at peace for once,' she reminded him, 'but the chances of repeating this will be even less when the baby comes.'

She hoped that he wasn't going to interpret that remark as lack of enthusiasm for further motherhood, as he'd done on previous occasions, but with the upbeat mood still upon him Piers just smiled and said easily, 'We've got the rest of our lives to do this kind of thing…haven't we?'

'Have we?' she asked in a low voice.

He didn't answer. The lights were dimming. The interval was over, and Kerry knew it would be hard to concentrate on the second act after what he'd just said. Yet she wasn't going to ask again. If he'd meant it, Piers would have to tell her so.

As the days went by Kerry was adjusting to a more restful lifestyle. She was missing the cut and thrust of A and E, but it was a relief not to be coming home tired after a day in Theatre and having to face household chores. Also there was time each evening to watch Piers transform a bedroom that wasn't in use for Rosalie to move into when the new occupant of the nursery arrived. It was all peaceful and domesticated and to a degree she was happy.

On the night when he was putting the last coat of paint on the woodwork of the bedroom, Piers said whimsically, 'When I boarded the homeward flight from New Zealand I never dreamt I was about to discover that I had a daughter and that in a few months' time I would be preparing for the arrival of child number two.'

He sounded contented. There'd been no barb in what he'd said. But instead of being happy at his mood, Kerry asked perversely, 'Why exactly *did* you come back?' It was a question that she'd wanted an answer to for a long time and suddenly the need to ask it was overwhelming.

Piers was on his knees, glossing the last piece of skirting-board. He looked up and she saw that his relaxed manner had gone.

'I came back for a few reasons,' he said evenly. 'Some much more important than others.' His glance went over the newly decorated bedroom. 'I would like to be able to say that one of them was because of my child, but it wouldn't be true as I didn't know she existed.'

'You may not have come out of hiding because of Rosalie,' Kerry countered, 'but she is the reason you've stayed, isn't she? That and the job.'

She was hurting inside, wanting him to say that *she* was the reason he'd returned.

'Yes, in part,' he agreed, and added, throwing her a crumb, 'but I also had a wife back here that I hadn't seen in a long time. I had no idea whether she'd found someone else or what, and being offered the job provided a chance to find out.'

'So you wouldn't have come back if it hadn't been for that?'

'I didn't say that, Kerry. I'd thought about it often. But it was my stupid pride that took me away from you, and it was the same thing that stopped me from coming back.

'When the offer of the job came up it seemed the ideal opportunity to return without losing face. I had intended finding myself somewhere to live and getting settled in on the trauma unit before I got in touch with you. I reckoned that by then I would have found out what was going on in your life and would know what my next move was. But it didn't turn out like that, did it? For one thing, Dad hadn't told me that I would be working with you at the hospital.

'If you remember, I hadn't been back in the UK more than a couple of hours when you were on the phone, demanding that I come round here straight away, and after that it all went haywire. You told me that my father was dead. I discovered that we had a child, and all my clever planning went out of the window.'

'So it was all about not losing face,' Kerry said slowly. 'You knew that our marriage was on a slippery slope and because you'd never been associated with failure before, you opted out. All the misery and heartache I've endured was because of your pride.'

'We were both headstrong and stubborn,' he pointed out. 'The marriage wouldn't have lasted much longer the way we were behaving. Your championing

of Cosgrove started it…and finished it. I couldn't believe that you didn't see through him.'

'I've admitted that you were right about him,' she
told him levelly. 'But your constant criticism wasn't
going to make him improve, was it?'

'No, it wasn't. But there was a lot of jealousy
mixed up with it, I'm afraid.'

'Why couldn't we have talked like this then,
Piers?' she said regretfully.

'I don't know. I really don't know.' He put the lid
back on the tin of paint, stripped off the overalls he'd
been wearing and said, 'I have to go. I've promised
Natalie that I'll call in at the refuge. They've had a
couple of cases of tuberculosis recently and the last
thing they want is something like that spreading
amongst them.'

He must be losing his grip, Piers was thinking as he
drove to the refuge. Why hadn't he told Kerry the
real reason why he'd come back? It had been because
he couldn't stand being away from her a moment
longer.

When he'd finally surfaced and rung his father,
he'd asked about her and Daniel had merely said that
Kerry was fine and staying with him. That had been
all, but it had told him that she wasn't living with
anyone who had stepped into *his* shoes. That if there
was anyone else in her life, they weren't living together.

The job offer had been coincidental. It was the fact
that though his father hadn't been very forthcoming
when he'd enquired after her, he had at least told him
that she could be found at his house, and that had

made him even more eager to return to London and end the lonely exile that he'd brought upon himself.

And so what had he just done? Because he was still wary of ruining the second chance that he'd been given, he'd made her think that she came low on the list of reasons why he'd come back. He was hedging and knew it, but he had to be certain that she wanted him back before he told her the truth.

When he'd gone Kerry thought, So much for that. They'd clarified some of the things she was curious about and that had been it. There had been some tying up of loose ends, rather than clearing the way for the future, but if Piers was satisfied with the present situation maybe he wasn't asking for more. Though it wasn't like him. She'd never known him be satisfied with half-measures before.

The ring still lay in the drawer and Kerry felt if she had the answer to it being there she might be able see the way ahead more clearly. But she was prepared to wait. No way was she going to ask Piers about it. If there was any first move to be made, he was the one who was going to have to make it.

Lizzie had stopped coming round to mind Rosalie for the present and was engaged in organising an exhibition of her paintings to be shown on Valentine's Day at the big library not far from where they lived.

They were a selection of oil paintings with romantic overtones, chosen to coincide with a display of books from some of the top romantic novelists, and amongst the paintings was going to be a surprise for a certain doctor and nurse.

She had found it amongst her collection from way back, a vibrant extravaganza in oils of Piers and Kerry, carefree and confident on their wedding day. They weren't to know it but they were about to receive a reminder of that day. She'd decided that a push in the right direction was what they needed. So the picture was going to be the focal point of the exhibition.

Kerry had offered to help with the preparations a few times, but on each occasion Lizzie had said firmly, 'There's no need. I've got the library staff here to assist.'

She didn't want her friend to see the picture until the day of the exhibition, and the same applied to Piers. She was hoping that they would come together in the evening, but could hardly insist on it. And in the way that the best-laid plans could go astray, Kerry turned up in the afternoon with just Rosalie.

She was smiling as she came through the door of the exhibition room. This was Lizzie's day and she was pleased for her. She had a lot of talent and the exhibition would enhance her reputation as an artist.

When Lizzie saw that Kerry was alone, she sighed. The impact, if any, wouldn't be the same if they weren't together.

'Where's Piers?' she asked, as Kerry prepared to view the paintings.

'Working, of course,' she said in mild surprise. 'He will be coming during the evening. Why?'

'No reason. I just thought that you might have come together.'

Kerry's glance was on what was in front of her,

and when Lizzie heard her gasp she knew that she'd seen the painting.

'Oh, Lizzie!' she breathed. 'Was that what we were like? I'd forgotten that you'd painted us.'

'It was you...and it still *is*,' Lizzie said determinedly. 'So do something about it!'

She was called away at that moment and Kerry was left to tour the exhibition on her own, but as she moved from one exhibit to another her glance kept returning to the wedding pair in the centre.

The bride with smooth tanned shoulders above a strapless bodice that belonged to a floating skirt of cream taffeta. And her dream man in a grey morning suit and topper, dashing and confident. Enough to make any woman's heart beat faster.

Where had they gone? she thought dismally. They'd been replaced by a pregnant mother whose feet were beginning to swell and a dedicated surgeon with tired lines round his eyes, who loved his child and kept his thoughts about his wife to himself.

Lizzie had said she should do something about it, but what? Piers seemed happy enough with the way they were.

'You're not mad at me for showing the painting, are you?' she asked anxiously as Kerry was about to leave.

'No, of course not,' she told her. 'I just can't believe that is how we were when I look at us now. We hadn't a care in the world in those days. I thought we'd be in love for ever.'

'I don't think that anything has changed regarding that. You both got sidetracked, took a wrong turning,' Lizzie insisted staunchly. 'From where I'm standing,

it seems that Piers is ready to be there for you every
step of the way...if you'll let him.'

'It would seem that we see my life through different eyes,' Kerry said dismally, and before she broke
down and wept she went.

Piers had decided to call in at the exhibition on his
way home that evening. It had been a depressing day
with what had seemed like half of those who went
around the city on two wheels ending up in Accident
and Emergency for one reason or another.

There had been two motorcyclists brought to the
unit from separate crashes where the car drivers had
escaped unhurt and the bikers had been seriously injured, and a teenage cyclist who'd been riding on the
pavement and had had to swerve to avoid an elderly
pedestrian. He had fallen off his bike and broken his
leg.

At the end of the day the success rate regarding the
injured trio had been one in Intensive Care, one in a
cast and one in the mortuary. The older of the two
bikers had been too badly injured to respond to their
desperate efforts and Piers had had to break the news
to his desolate family. He'd done it before and would
have to do it again, but it was always a terrible moment, bringing heartbreak to the relatives.

All of which was making him feel loath to have to
turn out again after he'd eaten. So calling in at the
exhibition on his way home had seemed like a good
idea. Until he heard an elderly lady say to her friend,
'Isn't that the man in the wedding painting?' And
realised that she was pointing at him.

182 A SURGEON'S MARRIAGE WISH

'Might be,' the other matron said, 'but he looks older, don't you think?'

What were they on about? he wondered, and then he saw it. Kerry and himself on their wedding day, confident, brash and beautiful.

They'd come a long way since then, he thought achingly, and he wouldn't want to change a moment of what he had now for what he'd had then.

'Has Kerry seen this?' he asked Lizzie.

'Yes. She came this afternoon.'

'And what did she have to say?'

'Er…not a lot. I think she was upset when she saw how you both used to be and didn't stay long.'

He was ready to leave himself. Couldn't wait to get home to her after seeing the picture. He'd waited long enough. The moment he got in he was going to give Kerry the ring, tell her that he loved her even more now than he had then and suggest they take their marriage vows again. If she refused the ring and didn't want a fresh start, at least he would have tried.

When he turned into the road where they lived he felt himself tensing behind the wheel. The house was in darkness at six o'clock on a dark February night. Where were his wife and daughter? Lizzie had said that they'd gone home in the late afternoon. Surely they hadn't ventured out again.

At this time the house was usually ablaze with light, with Kerry in the kitchen and Rosalie playing somewhere near. Don't panic until you have something to panic about, he told himself as he put his key in the lock.

As he stepped inside he collided with Rosalie's push-chair in the darkened hallway, and when he flicked the light switch on he saw that she was asleep in it. His anxiety increased, even though he knew that, wherever their child was, Kerry wouldn't be far away. But Lizzie had said that she'd left the exhibition in a distressed state after seeing the painting. Obviously its effect on her had been different from his. But surely she wouldn't want them to go back to those days, he thought as he moved quickly towards the darkened kitchen.

Once again he flicked on the light switch and she was there, seated at the table, gazing into space with a half-peeled carrot in her hand.

'Why are you sitting in the dark?' he asked gently. 'I was worried when I drove up and saw no lights on. Do you know that Rosalie is asleep in her push-chair in the hall?'

She nodded and said flatly, 'Yes. She dozed off on the way back from the exhibition, and as I needed time to think I didn't disturb her. I never noticed the daylight going.'

'You must have been sitting like that for ages, then.'

'Yes. I suppose I have,' she mumbled.

'Lizzie said you were upset when you saw the painting.'

'Mmm. I was. Weren't you?'

'No. Not at all. It made me realise how much I value what I have now.'

So far Kerry's manner had been lethargic, as if during that time in the dark she'd moved to somewhere out of reach, but now he had her attention.

'You can't mean that.'

'Yes, I do. After I'd seen the painting I couldn't get home to you quickly enough.'

'I would have thought it would have had the opposite effect. That you would want to get away.'

'Oh, Kerry!' he groaned. 'Everything I want is here.' He placed his hand lightly on her stomach. 'In there, asleep in the push-chair in the hall and seated at the kitchen table, peeling carrots. I've got something to give you that has been in the desk drawer for weeks while I've been waiting for the right moment.'

Her eyes brightened, the clouds lifting. 'It wouldn't be a ring, would it?' she breathed.

'Oh, no!' he exclaimed. 'Don't tell me that you knew it was there.'

'I found it when I was looking for gift labels on Christmas Eve.'

'So that's why you weren't ecstatic when I gave you your presents.'

'I was devastated, which I suppose served me right for taking it for granted that it was for me.'

'Kerry, darling,' he said softly, 'who else would it be for?'

'The woman with the tattoo?'

He laughed low in his throat. 'That was a joke as you should have known.'

'I didn't know *anything* when you came back into my life, except that miraculously you were there. I love you so much, Piers.'

'And I love you,' he said with a break in his voice.

'You say that and I believe you, but do you trust me, Piers? Do you believe that I was never unfaithful?'

'Yes, I do,' he assured her. 'Within hours of leaving you I knew that I was a jealous, stupid fool, but arrogance and pride wouldn't let me turn the car round. So I paid the price with endless months of misery.'

He touched her cheek tenderly. 'Don't go away. I'm going to get the ring, and once it's on your finger there is something I want to ask you.'

She smiled. 'I'm not going to go away. You're stuck with me now, and what more fitting day than St Valentine's to bring our love for each other out into the open at last?'

When the diamonds and pearls were glowing up at him on her finger, she said, 'So what do you want to ask me? This is usually the moment when the man asks the woman to marry him, but we've been there, done that.'

It was his turn to smile.

'You're thinking along the right lines. I'd like us to take our marriage vows again, if you are willing. I think we've grown up a bit since the first time, don't you?'

There were tears in her eyes.

'I can't think of anything I would want to do more, Piers. Let's do it before the baby arrives.'

And they did. On a cold Sunday morning they left the cosiness of the bed they were sharing and went to church with Rosalie wrapped up snugly against the cold. In front of the assembled congregation they repeated their marriage vows, with hands joined, eyes meeting and happiness there for all to see.

'There is just one thing missing to make life complete,' Piers said as they drove home after the service.

'You mean the baby,' Kerry said softly.

'I do indeed.'

'It won't be long now, Just a matter of days.'

'I know, and I feel truly blessed,' he told her.

When Daniel Valentine Jefferson came into the world he began to exercise his lungs immediately, and the man sitting beside the bed holding his wife's hand answered the question in her eyes as he told her joyfully, 'That's our son that you can hear, Kerry. We've got a beautiful boy.'

The midwife approached with the red-faced, protesting newborn, and when she placed him in his mother's arms Piers said in a low voice. 'I love you, Kerry. I always have and I always will.'

'I know,' she said softly, and hoped that their son's namesake would be smiling down on them from somewhere in eternity.

MILLS & BOON®

Live the emotion

AUGUST 2005 HARDBACK TITLES

ROMANCE™

The Brazilian's Blackmailed Bride *Michelle Reid*		
	H6228	0 263 18723 3
Expecting the Playboy's Heir *Penny Jordan*		
	H6229	0 263 18724 1
The Tycoon's Trophy Wife *Miranda Lee*	H6230	0 263 18725 X
Wedding Vow of Revenge *Lucy Monroe*	H6231	0 263 18726 8
Sale or Return Bride *Sarah Morgan*	H6232	0 263 18727 6
Prince's Passion *Carole Mortimer*	H6233	0 263 18728 4
The Mancini Marriage Bargain *Trish Morey*	H6234	0 263 18729 2
The Rich Man's Virgin *Lindsay Armstrong*	H6235	0 263 18730 6
Marriage at Murraree *Margaret Way*	H6236	0 263 18731 4
Winning Back His Wife *Barbara McMahon*	H6237	0 263 18732 2
Just Friends to...Just Married *Renee Roszel*		
	H6238	0 263 18733 0
The Shock Engagement *Ally Blake*	H6239	0 263 18734 9
To Kiss a Sheikh *Teresa Southwick*	H6240	0 263 18735 7
The Boss's Baby Surprise *Lilian Darcy*	H6241	0 263 18736 5
Bride by Accident *Marion Lennox*	H6242	0 263 18737 3
A Surgeon's Marriage Wish *Abigail Gordon*	H6243	0 263 18738 1

HISTORICAL ROMANCE™

The Marriage Debt *Louise Allen*	H606	0 263 18817 5
The Rake and the Rebel *Mary Brendan*	H607	0 263 18818 3
The Engagement *Kate Bridges*	H608	0 263 18948 1

MEDICAL ROMANCE™

Spanish Doctor, Pregnant Nurse *Carol Marinelli*		
	M523	0 263 18841 8
Coming Home to Katoomba *Lucy Clark*	M524	0 263 18842 6

0705 Gen Std HB

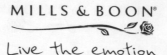

MILLS & BOON®

Live the emotion

AUGUST 2005 LARGE PRINT TITLES

ROMANCE™

Possessed by the Sheikh *Penny Jordan*	1791	0 263 18571 0
The Disobedient Bride *Helen Bianchin*	1792	0 263 18572 9
His Pregnant Mistress *Carol Marinelli*	1793	0 263 18573 7
The Future King's Bride *Sharon Kendrick*	1794	0 263 18574 5
Vacancy: Wife of Convenience *Jessica Steele*		
	1795	0 263 18575 3
His Hired Bride *Susan Fox*	1796	0 263 18576 1
In the Shelter of His Arms *Jackie Braun*	1797	0 263 18577 X
The Marriage Adventure *Hannah Bernard*	1798	0 263 18578 8

HISTORICAL ROMANCE™

Her Gentleman Protector *Meg Alexander*	304	0 263 18505 2
A Perfect Knight *Anne Herries*	305	0 263 18506 0
A Wild Justice *Gail Ranstrom*	306	0 263 18954 6

MEDICAL ROMANCE™

Emergency at Inglewood *Alison Roberts*	569	0 263 18471 4
A Very Special Midwife *Gill Sanderson*	570	0 263 18472 2
The GP's Valentine Proposal *Jessica Matthews*		
	571	0 263 18473 0
The Doctors' Baby Bond *Abigail Gordon*	572	0 263 18474 9

0705 Gen Std LP

MILLS & BOON®

Live the emotion

SEPTEMBER 2005 HARDBACK TITLES

ROMANCE™

The Disobedient Virgin *Sandra Marton*	H6244	0 263 18739 X
A Scandalous Marriage *Miranda Lee*	H6245	0 263 18740 3
Sleeping with a Stranger *Anne Mather*	H6246	0 263 18741 1
At the Italian's Command *Cathy Williams*	H6247	0 263 18742 X
Prince's Pleasure *Carole Mortimer*	H6248	0 263 18743 8
His One-Night Mistress *Sandra Field*	H6249	0 263 18744 6
The Royal Baby Bargain *Robyn Donald*	H6250	0 263 18745 4
Back in her Husband's Bed *Melanie Milburne*		
	H6251	0 263 18746 2
Wife and Mother Forever *Lucy Gordon*	H6252	0 263 18747 0
Christmas Gift: A Family *Barbara Hannay*		
	H6253	0 263 18748 9
Mistletoe Marriage *Jessica Hart*	H6254	0 263 18749 7
Taking on the Boss *Darcy Maguire*	H6255	0 263 18750 0
To Wed a Sheikh *Teresa Southwick*	H6256	0 263 18751 9
Major Daddy *Cara Colter*	H6257	0 263 18752 7
A Child To Call Her Own *Gill Sanderson*	H6258	0 263 18753 5
Coming Home for Christmas *Meredith Webber*		
	H6259	0 263 18754 3

HISTORICAL ROMANCE™

A Reputable Rake *Diane Gaston*	H609	0 263 18819 1
Conquest Bride *Meriel Fuller*	H610	0 263 18820 5
Princess of Fortune *Miranda Jarrett*	H611	0 263 18949 X

MEDICAL ROMANCE™

The Nurse's Christmas Wish *Sarah Morgan*		
	M525	0 263 18843 4
The Consultant's Christmas Proposal *Kate Hardy*		
	M526	0 263 18844 2

MILLS & BOON®

Live the emotion

SEPTEMBER 2005 LARGE PRINT TITLES

ROMANCE™

The Italian's Stolen Bride *Emma Darcy*   1799 0 263 18579 6
The Purchased Wife *Michelle Reid*   1800 0 263 18580 X
Bound by Blackmail *Kate Walker*   1801 0 263 18581 8
Public Wife, Private Mistress *Sarah Morgan*
    1802 0 263 18582 6
Their Pregnancy Bombshell *Barbara McMahon*
    1803 0 263 18583 4
The Corporate Marriage Campaign *Leigh Michaels*
    1804 0 263 18584 2
A Mother For His Daughter *Ally Blake*   1805 0 263 18585 0
The Boss's Convenient Bride *Jennie Adams*
    1806 0 263 18586 9

HISTORICAL ROMANCE™

A Model Débutante *Louise Allen*   307 0 263 18507 9
The Bought Bride *Juliet Landon*   308 0 263 18508 7
Raven's Vow *Gayle Wilson*   309 0 263 18955 4

MEDICAL ROMANCE™

His Longed-For Baby *Josie Metcalfe*   573 0 263 18475 7
Emergency: A Marriage Worth Keeping *Carol Marinelli*
    574 0 263 18476 5
The Greek Doctor's Rescue *Meredith Webber*
    575 0 263 18477 3
The Consultant's Secret Son *Joanna Neil*   576 0 263 18478 1

0805 Gen Std LP